The Darkness We Leave Behind

R.P.G. Colley

R.P.G. Colley

Fiction:

Love and War Series:

The Searight Saga:

The Darkness We Leave Behind

Rupertcolley.com

A Time to Say Hello

A Parisian suburb, October 1968

Henri Moreau stood at the mirror in the narrow hallway of his apartment, buttoning up his gabardine coat. Hetty, their tiny ginger cat, rubbed herself against his leg. It was a Friday morning, his favourite day of the week, the one day of the week he had somewhere to go, friends to meet. And, as a bonus, today he and Isabella were expecting a visit from their daughter and granddaughter. 'What time did you say they'd be here?'

His wife, in the bedroom, shouted through. 'For the hundredth time, Henri, around lunchtime, maybe early afternoon.'

'Excellent,' he said to himself, straightening his tie. Had she really said it a hundred times? Probably, yes.

Isabella had left the radio on in the kitchen. He could hear a reporter reporting from the Summer Olympics. It may have been October but it was still summer in Mexico. Isabella came through and joined him in the hallway. 'Why don't you invite your friends back here one day?'

What an awful idea, he thought. 'We're fine where we are. You look nice,' he said, changing the subject. She was wearing a green dress with a small blue cardigan he hadn't seen before.

'I'm meeting friends too. I'm sure I told you.' She took her coat and her wide-brimmed hat from the hat stand. 'I'm back to school Monday so might as well enjoy the freedom while I can.'

He patted his pockets, making sure he had his cigarettes and lighter and, just in case, a handkerchief. Hetty had disappeared.

'Have you heard the news, Henri?'

'About the Olympics, yes.'

'No, not the Olympics. About that court case.'

'What court case?'

She pushed him aside from the mirror and angled the brim of her hat. 'About the collaborator.'

'What about it?'

'Oh, nothing, Henri. Forget I mentioned it. You forget most things,' she added under her breath. 'Right, shall we leave together? I'm ready if you are.'

'Yeah. Sure.'

Together, they caught the lift down from the fourth floor to the ground.

The morning was cold; a moisture in the air, a sharp wind blew about the fallen leaves that had gathered on the pavements. Isabella always walked too fast for Henri and he had to make an effort simply to keep up. She waved at a couple of girls on bicycles he assumed were her pupils. He wanted to ask whom she was meeting but feared she'd already told him and that he'd forgotten – again. And anyway, he wasn't that interested. He'd only have been making conversation. His memory hadn't always been this bad. But he did remember Suzanne and Ruby were due at some point today. Did Isabella say lunchtime? He wasn't sure. He couldn't wait. He hadn't seen his granddaughter for six months. They lived down south in Aix-en-Provence, some seven hundred kilometres away. Ruby was six already. The same age as… No, he couldn't think it. But the comparison was natural; he did it all the time, he'd look into his little granddaughter's eyes and tried to see the resemblance. He tried to stop himself, but the pull was always too strong.

They were approaching the Metro station. Nearby, to the side of a small park, stood the statue of some nineteenth-century man in a long cloak, a former mayor of the borough, whose name Henri could never remember nor why he should merit a statue. In fact, no one knew but it had become a meeting point, and indeed Henri spied a man pacing on the sandy path in front of it, checking on his watch.

They reached the Metro station. 'Well, have a nice day,' said Henri.

'And you. Will you be OK?'

'Of course. Why shouldn't I be?'

Isabella pulled on the lapel of his coat. 'You know why.' She pecked him on the cheek, and descended into the station, throwing him a final glance over her shoulder. 'I'll see you this evening.'

Henri watched her trot down the steps. Yes, he thought, he knew why she'd asked him that. Isabella knew what he was thinking about. He thought about her every day, lived with that ache continually as if he had a stone permanently lodged in the pit of his stomach. Time didn't alleviate the pain; if anything, it seemed to magnify as he got older. And today especially, was hard, for today, the 17th October, would have been her birthday. Some things you never forget.

The cafe was just another two hundred or so metres further down the street. With hands in pockets, he looked up at the sky and the dark clouds scudding by. He heard a squeal of laughter; the man at the statue was hugging a woman with such intensity, he'd lifted her off the ground. Henri smiled as he sauntered along; how nice it must be to be that much in love, to be so overjoyed to meet someone. He passed his barbers, where he went every other Tuesday. Jacques, the barber, a dwarf, needed to stand on a wooden box but he knew his way around with a pair of scissors. Jacques caught Henri's eye and lifted the brim of an invisible hat by way of acknowledgement.

A couple of hardy men sat outside the Cafe du Flore. Inside, the cafe was half full, mainly of older men, like himself, mostly sitting by themselves, enjoying a cup of coffee and a cigarette, reading their newspapers. A couple of men were playing draughts, leaning forward in their chairs, deep in concentration. The radio played pop music in the background. He sidled across the black and white, two-toned floor and hung his coat and hat on the hat stand, glancing at himself in the large mirror bearing the Coca-Cola logo. 'Good morning, Jean,' he said to the waiter behind the counter. 'Am I the first?'

'No, monsieur, they're already here.'

Sure enough, Henri found his three friends sitting at their usual table in one of the booths, sitting beneath a low-hung lamp with a large floral-patterned shade. On the wall behind them, a large wooden plank depicting a painting of a multi-coloured cockerel. A copy of *Le Monde* lay folded on the table. 'Good morning, gents.'

He shook hands with his friends: Gustave Garnier, Roger Béart and Antoine Leclerc.

'Shall we order?' asked Garnier, pushing his glasses up his nose. 'The usual?' They agreed on the usual – black coffee and a large pastry each.

Jean, the waiter, took their order, committing it to memory.

Gustave Garnier had been a teacher, and, by his own admission, not a particularly good one. French literature was

5

his main subject, a connoisseur of nineteenth-century French poetry plus a bit of Shakespeare thrown in. He wore an ash-brown jacket with elbow patches, the patches lined with grease, and thick-rimmed brown glasses. He, like Moreau, was in his mid-fifties.

Roger Béart was a good fifteen years older than the other two. He'd fought with the French cavalry during the Great War, serving in the Palestinian desert. He wore his age like a badge of honour – his heavily lined face, his eyebrows too bushy, his moustache unkempt.

Antoine Leclerc, the youngest amongst them, a self-employed architect who, only occasionally, joined them on their Friday morning meet ups. The others, Henri Moreau included, were, by their own admission, grizzled old men while Leclerc still viewed life as exciting and anticipated the future with a degree of optimism.

'Have you seen this?' asked Béart, the older man. 'Two black athletes at the Olympics.' He pushed the newspaper across the table.

The front-page photograph showed three athletes on the podium, two of them black, both with their hands raised in the air, their heads bowed. 'Are they wearing gloves?'

'It's the black salute,' said Garnier. 'You know, black power and all that.'

'They're standing up for what they believe in,' said Leclerc,

6

the younger man. 'That takes courage, don't you think?'

'I don't see the point,' said Garnier.

'You don't see the point?' said Leclerc. 'Christ, man. If more people stood up like these men…'

'Like we should have, you mean.'

'Yeah, well. Maybe.'

'We can't all be heroes,' said Moreau.

A solitary cheer erupted from nearby. One of the men had won his game of draughts.

'Your coffees, gentlemen.' Jean deposited their coffees and pastries. 'You stay more than an hour, you have to buy more.'

'Don't you worry, young man,' said Béart.

Jean, who wasn't a day under sixty, raised an eyebrow. Tucking the tray under his arm, he saw the newspaper with the photo of the black athletes. 'They should strip them of their medals for that little show of defiance. Bloody blacks, you can't trust them.'

'Yeah, thanks, Jean. We'll call you when we need something.'

'Huh.'

They watched him retreat to the counter. Garnier took a knife and delicately cut into his pastry. 'Have you seen this other story, about the trial of that woman?'

'What woman?' asked Béart.

Garnier, picking up the newspaper, read aloud: '*Her victims*

7

called her 'The Lady with the Truncheon'; infamous for wielding her club against the Jewish inmates at the Nazi-run camp in the Parisian suburb of Drancy. For twenty-three years she has evaded justice but yesterday at Le Palais de Justice, sixty-eight-year-old Hilda Lapointe, a former guard at the wartime internment camp, was found guilty and sentenced to five years for maltreatment and war crimes.'

'Drancy? Did you... did you say Drancy?' asked Moreau.

'You heard. Have you not read about this? Christ, where have you been, Henri?'

'He lives under a rock,' said Béart.

'It's been front-page news all week,' said Garnier. 'Here...' He passed the newspaper to Moreau. Moreau glanced at the mug-shot photo of the woman.

'I've not heard about this. I think my wife mentioned it this morning but...' He folded the newspaper and left it on the table. He looked down at his plate, not wanting to look his friend in the eye.

'You all right, Henri?' asked Leclerc. 'Don't you like your pastry?'

'No, no, it's... I'm fine.'

'Five years?' said Béart. 'Is that all? Five years – that's sod all. She'll be out in three. If I had my way, I'd hang her, the bitch. Any Frenchman, or woman, who did the Nazi's work for them should be strung up, in my opinion.'

Now, it was Garnier's turn to avert his eyes. 'It's not always

8

black and white, you know, Roger.'

Béart made a *pfft* sound as he licked his fingertips.

'The interesting thing,' said Garnier, 'is that her friend, the music conductor, stuck up for her.'

'What music conductor?' asked Moreau.

'Can't remember his name. Everyone just calls him "The Maestro".'

'What did he say, this Maestro?'

'You can read it here. Basically, she helped him out during the war, so he stood up in court as a character witness for her.'

Béart laughed. 'Well, that's his career up the spout. Serves him right, the stupid bastard. I hope Hilda Lapointe appreciates the effort.'

'I doubt it,' said Leclerc.

Moreau took a second look at Hilda Lapointe's photograph. She looked so sure of herself, he thought, so hard, like a woman with an unforgiving soul. Her eyes bore into him, defiant, cold, calculating. He trembled slightly. Just looking at her gave him the jitters. He took a large gulp of coffee, and turning the newspaper over, looked back at the photo of the black athletes. He could cope with that; their picture didn't make his blood run cold, the word 'Olympics' didn't make his throat turn dry like hearing, or seeing, that most hateful of names – Drancy.

'Listen,' said Béart, jabbing the table with his finger, 'anyone who worked at Drancy was a bastard. That place was simply a holding camp for the Jews before they shipped 'em off to Auschwitz. Oh, the people who worked there can deny it as much as they want, but they knew, they bloody knew.'

Moreau shocked himself as much as his companions when he slammed his hand against the table. 'Stop, will you? Just stop talking about it, OK?'

Béart and Garnier exchanged knowing looks. 'Jeez, Henri, what's the matter?' asked Garnier.

'We've hit a raw nerve,' said Béart. 'That's what's the matter.'

'Just leave it, will you?'

Moreau felt a hand resting on his sleeve. It was Leclerc's. He didn't want it there, didn't want the young man's concern. 'Has something upset you, Henri? Is it all this talk about Drancy?'

'No, of course not.'

'I was there, you know, at Drancy. Were you at Drancy, Henri? Did you work there?'

'No!'

Béart shook his head.

Leclerc removed his hand from Moreau's sleeve. The four men sipped their coffees in silence, unable to look at each other. Béart lit a cigarette. Garnier turned the folded newspaper over and left it in the middle of the table, surrounded by their crumb-laden plates, the photo of Hilda Lapointe staring up at them.

A family of four came into the cafe, opening the door and bringing the cold inside with them, the two small girls at once lightening the atmosphere. They took a table near the door and the girls argued over who was sitting where. Dad slapped one, the nearest, on the thigh. The girl bit her bottom lip, trying hard not to cry while Mum admonished Dad, who threw his hands in the air with exasperation.

The draught players had packed up their game and now leant back in their chairs and talked over each other.

The father of the family tried to order but Jean kept shaking his head, as if saying they'd run out of *this* and run out of *that*. Moreau could sense the man's frustration, even at this distance.

Moreau then spoke. He hadn't planned it; in fact, he'd planned on saying absolutely nothing, but the words seemed to slip out of him, quietly, without fuss. 'Yes,' he said. 'I was at Drancy. Briefly. Not even a day but yes, I was there.'

He looked down at his lap but from the corner of his eye, he could see Garnier and Béart exchange looks again. Béart tapped his temple.

'You don't have to tell us, Henri,' said Leclerc.

'Why not?' said Béart. 'If he wants to, let him. I mean, how long have we been meeting here?'

11

Moreau looked at him and realised the man was sweating, his skin glistening under the weak light bulb of the lamp. 'Long enough,' he said.

'Exactly. We know each other of old–'

'But are we friends?' asked Leclerc. 'Truly? You don't even like us, Roger.'

Béart laughed. 'Antoine, you're a sentimental fool. And you, Gustave, I've met tadpoles with more backbone than you–'

'Thanks.'

'But what am I but an embittered old bastard living on my own, with no one to talk to from day to day? So, are you my friends?' He looked from Moreau to Garnier to Leclerc. 'Yeah, you're my friends. And why? Because we each have something missing in us,' he said, thumping his heart. 'We have much in common with this conductor fellow, this Maestro. He's one of the most famous men in France but he still can't break from what happened to him during the war. And now it's destroyed him. We are all widows – or widowers – of the war, each one of us. Though, for me, it wasn't the last war that undid me, but the one before. The result is the same. So, the three of us, sometimes four, we meet here every Friday and we talk and talk, and I look forward to it. But you know nothing about the gaping hole where my heart used to rest, and I know nothing of yours, Moreau, or you, Garnier. But it's there. I know it; we all know it. But we never give voice to it. And you know, I reckon this conductor might be happier now than ever. Yes, his reputation's been destroyed, but perhaps this trial has finally released him from his demons. And I reckon it's time we released ourselves from our demons too.'

'What are you saying, Roger?' asked Garnier.

'We confess.'

'Confess?'

'Yes. It takes a man who's been eaten from the inside to see it in another. We sit here every week and have done so for years. I declare the time has come.'

'My God, man, you're right,' said Leclerc. 'What do you say, Henri?'

'My granddaughter's arriving tonight. Or lunchtime, I can't remember now.'

'So?'

'If she knew, if my daughter knew what I did, they'd never speak to me again.' He twisted a napkin around his fingers. 'But you're right. I'll tell you my story; that is if you're sure.'

Béart nodded. Garnier smiled. 'Perhaps we should order another round of coffee first before Jean chucks us out.'

13

The Postman's Story

16 July 1942. Henri Moreau, as was his routine at eight in the morning, was on his bicycle delivering the post. He'd already been working for an hour and a half. It was a bright summer's morning, the sky sapphire blue. People waved at him. The sight of the postman doing his daily round was a reassuring presence. They thought his job an easy one; a pleasant, sociable way of earning one's living. A job that could be done and dusted by lunchtime each day. They didn't appreciate that Moreau had to be up and out of bed at half five every morning, six days a week, fifty-two weeks a year. It wasn't so bad this time of year, but all those cold, early starts during winter were tiresome indeed. They didn't see him cycling around in the dark, often in the rain, cold and sleet, while they were still tucked up in bed or enjoying a warm breakfast in front of the fire. They didn't realise the heaviness of his post-sack and the physical strain it put on his ageing shoulders. And the job came

with a responsibility. People, businesses, shops – they didn't appreciate how dependent they were on him doing his job and doing it well. The one time, the one single time, he dropped a letter, it was found by some snot-nosed school kid and handed in to the post office. And then there was hell to pay. But what really irked was when people accused him of being a collaborator because he had to deliver the German post. Post was post as far as he was concerned.

On the whole, though, Henri Moreau was pleased with life. The German occupation, painful though it was to see, was bearable, and life at home was cosy. But he was concerned, deeply concerned, because his wife was Jewish, and therefore, by default, so was his daughter, the six-year-old Marguerite. They'd been married ten years, he and Liliane (Lilly), and, if truth be told, it was only Marguerite that kept them together. Until recently, his wife's Jewishness was not something that had worried him. Nor anyone else. She was just a Frenchwoman, Marguerite just a French kid. Then came the Germans. Yet the Germans in this neck of woods had been more relaxed than their urban cousins, so although conscious of the Jewess he'd married, it wasn't a problem. But things had changed. Six months previously, the edict had come from the government – all Jews were compelled to wear a yellow star upon their clothing, with the word *Juif* clearly written upon it. Those who didn't and were caught out faced harsh

16

punishment. Now, people who had been pleasant enough to Lilly turned their backs on her or walked to the other side of the street with their noses in the air, as if offended by an unpleasant smell; Marguerite was shunned at school, made to sit at the back, avoided at playtime. He was no anti-Semitic, he told himself, but nonetheless... Nonetheless, he couldn't help feeling *ashamed* somehow. Ashamed that he had married a Jew.

On this particular warm July morning, Moreau, wearing a pair of shorts and a collared shirt unbuttoned at the top and his postman's cap, cycled the one kilometre from home to the post office, picked up his post sack, exchanging pleasantries, as always, with the postmistress, then made a start on his deliveries. Just like any other morning these last twelve years. Only this morning was slightly different. Today was the first day of the school holidays. Marguerite was beside herself with excitement – no more school for a whole two months, no more going to bed early, a whole summer to play with her friends in the streets, at least the ones she could still consider her friends. But the start of the summer holidays wasn't the only reason why this morning was to be different. This morning would see Henri Moreau's life, as he knew it, come to an end.

It was still only eight o'clock; Moreau was about a quarter through his deliveries. There was something odd in the air; he could feel it, and whatever it was he didn't like it. Turning into a wide residential street, still in the shade, he heard noises – it sounded like screaming. A green and cream-coloured bus had parked on the side of the street, and some policemen emerged – no, not some, but lots of them. So many police. Braking to a halt, Moreau wondered what sort of criminal lived in the town to warrant such a huge number of policemen. He saw a man in a black jacket pushed to the ground, his beret flying off, shouting. With his hands over his head, the man cowered as a cop hit him on the back with his truncheon. Moreau let slip the sack from his shoulder where it fell onto the road with a heavy, dull thud. A moment later, a woman appeared from the house, a policeman on either side, screaming, her face full of terror. Passers-by rushed away. A couple stopped next to Moreau – near enough to see what was happening but at a safe distance. Another policeman, this one carrying a bawling child, appeared. The woman screamed for her child. A cop hit her in the stomach, doubling her over. Moreau and the others flinched.

'What's happening?' asked Moreau, more to himself.

A man to his left said, 'Haven't you heard? They're arresting all the Jews.'

Then Moreau saw it – the familiar yellow star bright on the man's black jacket. There were other cops at the entrance of the bus. The man, woman and child, all three crying, were dragged towards the bus and one by one physically forced up the steps and pushed inside.

'They're arresting the Jews?' asked Moreau, his heart thumping, thinking of his daughter. 'Even the children? Why? What have they done?'

'I know, it's despicable, isn't it?'

In a shrill voice, a woman to his right said, 'It serves them right, if you ask me; bloody parasites.'

Moreau turned to look at her. She was a respectable, well-dressed woman; the sort of person who, before the war, would never have thought, let alone say, such a thing.

Back at the end of 1940, the French authorities had made all Jews register themselves. Moreau had dutifully gone along on the appointed day and registered his wife and daughter. He was regretting it now.

The cops were running, their feet heavy on the cobbles, disappearing down a narrow side street.

'Where are they going now?' asked Moreau, although he knew the answer.

'They know where all the Jews live,' said the man.

'Good,' said the woman. 'They should've done this years ago.'

'Oh my God.' He felt quite dizzy for a moment. The world seemed to move out of focus.

'Are you OK, buddy?' asked the man.

'What?' Marguerite. Something invisible seemed to be

19

choking him, squeezing his throat. 'I've got to go...' he said breathlessly. Clumsily, he turned his bicycle around, facing the way he'd just come. He had to get home. Before it was too late.

Cycling off, he heard the man shout after him. 'Oi, wait, you forgot your post.'

'He can't just leave it here,' came the woman's shrill voice.

Henri Moreau had been on his bicycle every day, bar Sundays, for years and years. Yet he had never, until this moment, ridden it with any speed. But by God, he did now. Standing up on the pedals, he sped down the streets, round corners and sharp bends, the wrong way down a one-way street, past the shops, overtaking slow-moving cars, a horse and cart, and other cyclists. He passed another family of Jews, screaming, hysterical, being hauled out of their homes by a different set of policemen. He kept going, the breeze causing his eyes to water, his heart pounding with exertion and fear. He could hear sirens, more shouting, a car screeching to a halt, a motorbike and sidecar. Everything was happening around him, but still, he pressed on. No one noticed the postman racing past them on his bicycle.

Eventually, he came to his street. No police here – yet. Thank God for that. He lived not far from the centre of town in a four-storey two-bedroom apartment that overlooked a cobbled courtyard. He took the corner into the courtyard at full speed, under an archway, skidding dramatically to a halt. Leaving his bike prostrate on the ground, its front wheel still spinning, he leapt off and ran inside. Panting heavily, he ran into the lobby, past the rows of metal post boxes, sidestepping Madam Blanchet, the concierge, her sleeves rolled up, a bucket of water cradled in the crook of her arm. 'Everything OK, Monsieur Moreau?' she asked in her sharp tone. Ignoring her, the postman bounded up the darkened stairs, taking two steps at a time, reaching the fourth floor.

Fumbling for his keys, aware of the sweat dripping from his every pore, he pushed open the front door. Slamming it closed behind him, he called out. 'Lilly! Marguerite!' No answer. The apartment seemed strangely quiet. No one in the kitchen; no one in the sitting room – Marguerite's toys scattered everywhere, as always, a doll here, a teddy there. His heart stopped – oh Lord, they've been taken. 'Please, no.' He called their names again, hearing the panic within his voice. Trying to catch his breath, he darted back to the kitchen, as if he might have missed them the first time, back to the sitting room, both bedrooms. Everything seemed in place; no sign of a struggle; Marguerite's favourite teddy bear, Lanky, with its red and yellow pullover, flopped on her pillow where she left it every day; the breakfast things stacked away, all in order. He tried to think – where could they be at this time of morning? Madam Giono – he'd ask his neighbour. Leaving the front door ajar, he darted out into the corridor and knocked furiously on his neighbour's door. Madam Giono, the young Italian widow, whom he'd always had a soft spot for, answered, concerned by Moreau's frantic knock. 'Good God, Henri, is there a fire?' She held a comatose black cat to her bosom.

'Madam Giono–'

'Isabella, please.'

'Isabella. Have you seen Lilly or Marguerite?' he asked in a rush, conscious of his breathlessness but still, even at this moment, aware that, as always, she looked divine in her silk dressing gown. 'Have you s-seen them?'

'No, should I have? Is everything OK, Henri?' She ran a finger down the lapel of his postman's jacket.

God, she was sexy. 'Has anyone called for us? Did you hear anything?'

'No. Why, should–'

'Thanks,' he said. 'Sorry, Madam Giono, Isabella, must rush. You look lovely by the way.'

'Why, thank you, Henri,' she said, stroking the cat.

He'd go out, look for them. No, what if they returned in the meantime? He had to stay, had to wait for them. Where in the hell were they? Where could they have gone? He felt weak with dread, so much energy, but nothing he could do. From one room to another, he paced up and down feeling like a caged

22

animal, trapped and afraid, very afraid.

From outside, he heard an engine. Looking out the kitchen window, his heart jumped on seeing the motorbike and sidecar pull up within the courtyard. Parking up in the street, beyond the archway, he saw the green and cream bus, several French police disembarking. He pulled away from the window, his breath coming in quick bursts. Then, at the same moment, he heard the key in the door – they were back. Lilly came running into the apartment, her coat flapping, dropping a bag of groceries in the hallway, Marguerite behind her. 'Henri,' she cried. 'What do we do?'

'I… I don't know.'

'They're outside. There's no escape.'

'Lock the door. Double lock it.'

'Papa, what's happening?'

'I'm not sure, s-sweetheart. It's probably nothing to worry about.'

'So why's Maman crying?'

'I'm not crying, love,' said Lilly, trying to hide the fear in her voice. 'Come, let's go sit down. Maybe a bit later we can make a start on that jigsaw puzzle of yours.'

Henri watched her remove her coat, saw her grimace at the hated star. Stuffing it in the little cupboard in the hallway, she turned to him, her face red with tears. 'There's nothing we can do, is there? We're trapped like rats.'

He didn't know how to answer. Then they heard it – the footsteps on the stairs, dozens and dozens of them, so it seemed, footsteps on the landing, coming to a halt outside their door. A moment of silence. Then the loud rap against the door. 'Police. Open up,' came the voice from outside.

Marguerite reached for her mother's hand. Henri put his finger to his lips. Another knock, even louder. 'Open up. All Jews are subject to arrest.'

'What's arrest mean, Maman?' whispered Marguerite.

'They... they just want to talk to us.'

The knocking on the door continued, on and on, a constant pounding.

'Make them stop,' said Lilly, her hands over her ears.

'I don't know what to do. I'm s-sorry.'

Grabbing him by his shirt, she said, 'Don't desert us, Henri Moreau. Do whatever you have to do, just save us. And if you can't...' Wiping away her tears, she continued, 'if you can't save me, save... save her.'

He tried to speak but managed only to nod, biting his lip, desperately trying not to cry in front of their daughter.

The knocking suddenly stopped. Moreau held his breath, knowing they were still on the landing.

'What's that noise?' asked Marguerite, hiding behind her mother, clutching her skirt, her voice barely audible.

It took him a few seconds to work it out. 'They're unlocking the door.'

Lilly clenched shut her eyes. 'Madam Blanchet – she's given them the key. The bitch.'

And then they were there; the door bursting open, a man in a trench coat in their hallway, two uniformed men behind him in their peaked hats and capes. 'Monsieur Moreau?' asked the officer, holding up a piece of paper.

Moreau couldn't speak.

Marguerite gripped onto her mother's skirt. Lilly reached back, taking her daughter's hand. 'What is it you want?' she asked, unable to hide the quiver in her voice.

'Madam Moreau? You are all under arrest.'

'Not the child,' said Moreau. 'S-surely not the child.'

'All three of you.'

The two men in uniforms sidled behind them, dark faces under their peaked hats, set mouths.

'You,' said the officer, pointing at Lilly. 'Pack a small case for all three of you. Essentials only. You have two minutes.'

She hesitated as if she didn't understand the instruction.

'Go on, now!' he shouted.

Spurred into action, she took Marguerite by the hand and raced to the bedroom, the uniforms following her.

Left alone with the officer, Moreau had to speak. Glancing behind at the bedroom, he turned and whispered, 'You can't arrest me. My wife's Jewish but I'm not.'

The officer frowned. 'You're not?'

'Look, my coat.' Retrieving his coat from the cupboard, he twisted and turned it in order to show the officer the breast pocket where the yellow star *would* have been.

'Doesn't prove much. Anyway, you're on my list so there's nothing I can do. You can speak to someone later down the line; try and sort it out.'

'What about them?'

'No way out of that. But you – for sure. Where are your papers?'

He would've shown the man but just at that point Lilly and Marguerite returned, a small black suitcase in Lily's hand; Lanky, the teddy bear, in Marguerite's.

'Here, let me,' said Moreau, reaching for the case.

With their coats on, the six of them marched down the stairs, the officer in front, the two uniforms at the rear. Between the first floor and the ground, they overtook Madam Giono descending the stairs. She pinned her back to the wall, her mouth gaping open, as the Moreaus and their escort passed by. No one spoke but Moreau felt his face flush red; he hadn't wanted her to see his moment of humiliation. At the bottom of the stairs, watching them descend, was Madam Blanchet, wiping her hands on her apron, an impish smile plastered on her pinched face.

Outside, the Moreaus were pushed towards the waiting bus.

Glancing behind, Henri Moreau saw his bicycle lying on the cobbled courtyard. So many people won't get their letters today, he thought; I've let them all down.

*

The bus was packed with Jews, most carrying bags or small cases. Young and old, grandparents, the decrepit, babes in arms, Jews together, crying, pointlessly pleading to each other, not knowing their fate.

Their town passed them by – the familiar streets, the shops, the apartment blocks, the cafés, the post office, the library, people going about their everyday business unaware that the bus driving by was full of desperate, frightened people. Moreau wondered if he'd ever see his town or his home again. The ride on the bus was brief, no more Jews to pick up – the Moreaus were the last. Ten minutes after leaving the Moreaus, they were at the train station. The station car park was full of green and cream buses, hundreds of Jews disembarking, all with their yellow stars, all but Henri Moreau, a heavy police presence surrounding them. A train awaited, the sun glinting off its engine, already emitting bellows of steam in preparation for departure.

Henri Moreau never realised there were so many Jews living in his town, until he heard someone say they were from another town about ten kilometres north. So, that explains it, he thought; the police had cast their net far and wide. Everyone, each and every one of them, looked small and diminished. There was crying, for sure, pitiful weeping, but no one was protesting, as if they all knew to do so was futile. The police merely had to herd them onto the trains, no one had to be forced, no coercion was needed. Lambs to the slaughter.

Marguerite held onto her mother's hand, Lilly to his. He would have tried to reassure them, but it was pointless. What could he, even as a Gentile, do in the face of this barbaric efficiency? He wanted to scream, 'I'm not a Jew! I'm not a bloody Jew!' Back at the apartment, the officer had said he should speak to someone. But there was no one to speak to, no one in charge. Perhaps if he could get inside the station, the ticket hall or somewhere, he'd find someone to speak to, someone with authority. As he took the steps onto the train, his hand momentarily let go of hers. 'Henri, please,' she cried, her hand reaching out for him.

'I'm s-sorry,' he muttered. He knew with a sudden, prophetic certainty that as long as they stuck together, he was as good as dead. He'd once loved her, and perhaps, in some way, he still did, but not enough to forfeit his life. Not enough. He had to do something to lose her.

Marguerite suddenly let out an ear-piercing scream. 'Lanky! I've lost Lanky.'

'Henri,' urged Lilly. 'You have to find Lanky.'

'What?'

Marguerite burst into tears.

'Yes, of course.' Pushing someone aside, he jumped off the steps.

He could see the bear on the ground, trampled in the dirt, but a policeman was on him in an instant. 'Oi, what're you doing?'

'My daughter, she's dropped...'

'Get back on,' said the cop reaching for his holster.

'Papa...'

'It's just there...'

'Henri, hurry...'

'It'll only take a minute.' Sidestepping the policeman, he managed to grab the bear. Turning back, he didn't see it coming, aware only of staggering back, falling to his knees, of the shooting pain over his eye.

Groaning, his hand over his eye socket, Moreau got up, clutching onto the bear.

People let him pass as he climbed up the train steps to join Lilly and Marguerite at the top, Lilly stroking her daughter's hair. 'Here,' he said, his eye throbbing with pain. 'Take it.'

'Thank you, Papa.'

'Thank you, Henri.'

They were among the first on board; the first into an empty carriage. Having put their suitcase and their coats on the overhead rack, they sat down. Within seconds, every other seat was taken, and Marguerite, holding onto Lanky, had to sit on her mother's lap in order to allow an elderly woman a seat. A man in a brown suit, sitting opposite, passed Moreau his handkerchief while Lilly used hers to wipe away Marguerite's tears and blow her nose. Moreau thanked him, daubing his swollen eye.

By the time the train left, some twenty minutes later, every seat in every compartment was taken; people were standing squashed in the gangways, the smell of sweat and fear everywhere. And so much noise – babies, children and adults crying, whimpering, people asking each other, 'Where are we going, where are they taking us?' Some commotion was taking place in the next-door carriage – some man trying to jump out of the window. No chance, thought Moreau, you couldn't squeeze a rabbit through that. Idiot.

Marguerite had fallen asleep on her mother's lap, sucking her thumb, a habit she'd broken a good year back. Moreau kissed his daughter's head and breathed in her smell. He knew what he was trying to do, he wanted to change his own mind, to persuade himself that whatever her fate, this little girl, he should share it. He stroked her cheek. She smiled in her sleep.

Leaning towards him, Lilly whispered in his ear. 'Henri, there must be something we can do. I married a Gentile; that must count for something. Find someone; get us out of here.'

He nodded.

Rising from his seat, he took his coat from the rack.

Lilly pulled a face as if to say, 'why do you need that?'

Pretending not to understand, he said 'excuse me' numerous times as he pushed his way out of the carriage and down the corridor. 'The toilets are blocked, chum,' said someone.

'I'll give it a go,' he said in return. 'Excuse me. Sorry. Excuse me.'

Finally, he found a policeman standing guard between two carriages.

'Excuse me.'

'Get back.'

'Listen, there's been a mistake.' Lowering his voice, he said, 'I'm not a Jew.'

'So?'

'Look,' he said, showing the man his coat. 'No s-star.'

'Nothing I can do. Now get back.'

'Can't I…'

'No. I'm not going to tell you again.'

Back in his carriage, a woman in a headscarf had taken his place. Lilly shrugged her shoulders in a "what could I do" gesture. 'Well…?' she mouthed.

He shook his head.

She sighed and turned her attention to the countryside

rushing past outside, squeezing Marguerite closer to her bosom.

*

An hour later, the train finally slowed down and came to a halt. The words 'where are we?' were on everyone's lips.

'Out, out, out!' shouted the policemen. 'Hurry up, out, out, out.'

Collecting their belongings, they were herded off the train, shoved through the ticket hall and marched down a bleak, deserted street with few buildings, the pavement full of potholes. The smell of cut grass wafted through the air. What a lovely smell, thought the postman, the smell of normality, of freedom. The silence of so many people, thought Moreau, is an oppressive noise, just the shuffle, shuffle, shuffle of so many feet. The name of the street, he noticed, was Rue de la Liberté. Carrying the suitcase, he felt hot wearing his coat on such a warm day. Eventually, they came to what looked like a huge residential multi-storey complex, a very modern if ugly piece of architecture. The same word filtered down the unending line of Jews making people shake with alarm – *Drancy*. Drancy. The word was enough to strike fear in the stoutest of hearts. This was the government's biggest concentration camp for Jews, northeast of Paris. Rumours about the place had circulated for years – about trains coming

32

to take them away from here, taking them to faraway places from which no one ever returned. People slowed down. 'Hurry, hurry,' shouted the policemen, pushing the odd Jew along. 'Get on there.'

Lilly squeezed Moreau's hand. 'Henri, I'm frightened.'

'I know. S-so am I.'

'Don't be frightened, Maman. I'll look after you.'

Despite herself, Lilly managed a laugh mixed in with her tears. 'Oh, my little love, I know you will.'

Approaching, the main gates loomed large; beyond the gates, a large, mud-packed yard, surrounded on three sides by these futuristic-looking apartment blocks. And everywhere, French police in their capes, swinging their truncheons. The noise was intense, the screaming of the adults, the wailing of the children, the shouting of policemen. They crowded into the yard, hundreds of them, Jews with their stars on their coats, pushed together like so many sheep, the sun beating down on their heads. Many were tired after the journey and the constant state of nervousness, especially the elderly, but the police wouldn't let them sit, forcing them to their feet, kicking them. 'Please let me sit,' said one woman, no more than twenty, 'I'm pregnant.' The policeman grabbed her by her hair, yanking her up. Her face crumpled into tears, as she supported the weight of her bulging belly. An older woman put her arm around her. The pregnant girl sobbed into her

33

shoulder.

Marguerite also was crying. Lilly picked her up and kissed her wet face. 'We'll stick together.' She looked at her husband. 'Won't we, Henri?'

It was as if she knew.

The booming voice through the loud hailer caught everyone's attention. They were about to be told something. 'Messieurs, Mesdames.' Moreau couldn't see where the voice was coming from but he could hear it all right. 'Messieurs, Mesdames, listen carefully, please. You are now at the Drancy detention centre. As Israelites, you are here under the direct orders of the Vichy authorities. The length of your stay here is yet to be determined. Each one of you has been allocated a space within the centre. The running of this camp is heavily regimented, and you will be expected to obey all rules, which will be relayed to you presently. The slightest infringement of any rule will be dealt with most severely. You have been warned. There are separate accommodation blocks for men and for women and… for children.'

It was almost as if this dismembered voice was expecting it – the pause before saying the words 'for children'. The spontaneous scream shattered the silence as mothers, wetting themselves, knowing their worst fear had come, clung to their children. And then it started. Police came charging in, wielding their batons, pulling mothers from children. The women, seized by primaeval reflexes, impervious to the punches and brutality of the police, desperately trying to hold onto their children. Lilly, her face white, beside herself, clung onto Marguerite, squeezing the life out of the screeching child. Henri tried to shield them, knowing it was a pointless task. Fists flew, batons swung, children thrown onto the dirt, mothers on their knees, their skirts covered in dried mud, hysterical; the air filled with screaming, a wall of screaming. A figure in black punched Lilly in the mouth. She fell back, losing her grip on Marguerite. The policeman made a grab for the girl. With eyes like those of the devil, Lilly leapt forward, lunging at him, pulling at his hair, knocking his hat off, scratching his face, drawing blood. Trying to scoop Marguerite up with one hand, he fought Lilly off, ripping the buttons from her dress. Moreau, shouting 'No!', pulled manically at his arm, trying to free Marguerite from his grasp. A sudden, unexpected blast of water threw them apart. Moreau found himself face down in the sodden dirt. Staggering to his feet, he searched for them among the wailing desperate women, the water knocking people down like bowling pins. He saw her, saw Lilly, on the ground, her hair soaked, her face and chest caked in mud, her arms seizing the policeman's legs. He called out her name, his voice lost amidst the screaming. Something smashed onto the back of his head. His eyes glazed. The intensity of the primordial noise clouded over. Swaying, he could see the blurred outline of his wife on her feet, hitting the back of the policeman as the man gripped his daughter by her midriff; Marguerite, kicking her legs, bellowing for help, reaching out for her.

And then everything went black.

*

Henri Moreau opened his eyes. What was that filthy smell? It took a few seconds for his eyes to focus but the memory of what had happened came to him in an instant. Lilly and Marguerite – where were they? He tried lifting himself up but fell back again as the piercing pain shot through his head, his eye still hurt from where the revolver had smashed into him. Checking his pockets, he still had the handkerchief the man on the train had given him. He was in a bed covered by a thin, scratchy blanket. Sitting at the end of the bed a gaunt man in spectacles, his beard turned yellow, biting his nails. They seemed to be in a dormitory of some sort, hundreds of men, the sound of a hundred quiet conversations. His throat felt dry, he realised just how thirsty he was. Clutching his head, gagging on the smell of decay and desperation, he swung his legs off the bed.

'Good morning,' said the bearded man. 'I'm afraid you missed breakfast.'

'Breakfast?'

'Oh yes, my friend.' The man counted the items on his fingers. 'We had sausages, a boiled egg, croissant, fresh ones, mind you, mushrooms, they were to die for, tomatoes and black coffee, very sweet.'

'What?'

'OK, I exaggerate – it was a small piece of rock-hard bread and black tea. Hello, my name is Mirabeau, Gabriel Mirabeau,' he said, offering his hand. 'Your eye's a mess.'

The man wore small, rounded spectacles, had bushy eyebrows and had, thought Moreau, a reassuring smile. 'Henri Moreau. I'm a postman – at least I was until yesterday. So, it wasn't all a dream then.'

'Sadly not. It really happened. The French really have turned on their own people, doing the Germans' dirty work for them. To think I used to be proud to call myself a Frenchman. Not any more.'

'They took the women and children.'

'Yes, we're all being kept separately.'

'Did they s-say anything else? How long they intend to keep us here.'

Mirabeau laughed. 'Henri – may I call you Henri? I've been here six months and I know nothing, except…'

'Except?'

'You've just arrived. Maybe it'd be too much to tell you.'

'Tell me.' It was obvious he wanted to.

'They send people off on trains. Where no one knows. But rumoured to be east, way out somewhere in Poland. And I don't reckon... They say they kill them there with gas.'

'Gas? That's... that's ridiculous.'

'You would've thought so.'

They sat in silence for a while, Moreau massaging his head, pressing the handkerchief to his eye. Already he was becoming accustomed to the stench of so many dirty men thrown in together. It seemed strange to think Lilly and Marguerite were close by but so far out of reach. He needed a drink, water, anything, something to eat. He wanted a bath, a shave; he needed to feel clean. He realised Lilly had made a mistake packing all their things into one case – for now, he had nothing, no clean pair of underpants, no toothbrush, no soap, nothing. Good God, they keep pigs in better conditions than this. The minutes ticked by, the hours. He wandered around a bit, so many men, so many stripped of their individuality, reduced to filthy, hungry animals, their every thought consumed by nothing but the most basic needs. Returning to his space, he asked Mirabeau what people did all day.

'Nothing,' came the reply. 'Nothing to do but worry. Oh, we have roll call first thing and they let us out for a bit of fresh air in the afternoons. They worry in case we all get TB or dysentery or something.'

'I'm not even a Jew,' said Moreau.

Mirabeau's large eyebrows knotted in puzzlement. 'You're not a Jew?' he said slowly. 'I don't understand, so what are you doing here?'

'I don't know. An administrative oversight, I guess.' He didn't mention Lilly.

'My God, man, then you're saved,' said Mirabeau, slapping him on his knee. 'Have you spoken to someone about this?'

'I've tried but I keep getting palmed off.'

'Do you have your papers?'

'Of course,' he said, checking his inside pocket.

'All you have to do…. No, that might not work. Now that you're in here, they might be happy to let you rot. We have to think.'

After a while, Mirabeau put his finger up. 'Got it,' he said. 'Tell them you've got TB. Like I said, they're terrified of it – you'll be out of here in a jiffy.'

'Tuberculosis? What do you mean? Surely, if it's that easy, why doesn't everyone do it; why don't you do it?'

'Because we're Jews. A Jew with TB? Best thing is a bullet. But you'd get away with it. Oh, Henri, I'm so happy to have met you. You've got to get out of here. If I can go to my death knowing I've saved a man, just one man, I'd be very happy.'

Moreau thought of Lilly. *Don't desert us. Do whatever you have to do, just save us. And if you can't save me, save her.* He shook his head, trying to rid himself of the memory.

'Henri? Henri, listen to me. Rub your face hard with your hands – again and again until your skin is bright red. Then bite your tongue until it bleeds. It'll be hard but you must do it. Then holler for a guard. Trust me, you'll be out of here by nightfall.'

Mirabeau was right – the biting of one's tongue was hard. But with his new friend's urging, he finally managed it. Mixed with his spittle, Moreau was surprised at the amount of blood he'd managed to produce.

'Well done,' said Mirabeau. He shook his hand. 'You're as red as a beetroot. I'm sorry to be losing you already but out you go, my friend. I wish you all the luck in the world. Are you married?'

'No.' He said it without hesitation.

'Excellent. Get out of here, live, and make love to as many women as you can.'

'Thank you,' said Moreau, putting on his coat. 'I'll never forget you.'

The man smiled, exposing his rotting teeth. 'Go now. Call for a guard.'

Moreau staggered through the dormitory, his hand at his mouth, crying in pain. He never knew he could act so well. He pounded at the wrought iron gates at the end of the dormitory. 'Guard, guard. Help!'

A man appeared, short and plump, not a policeman but still

a Frenchman in prison officer uniform. 'Get back. What is it? What's all this noise?'

'I'm ill, truly,' said Moreau breathlessly. 'TB.'

The guard stared at him for a moment, his eyes widening on seeing Moreau's red face, his bloodied eye and his bleeding mouth. 'Shit.' Calling over his shoulder, he shouted, 'Faure, I need some help here.'

The man called Faure appeared. 'Look at him,' said the first guard, pointing at Moreau. 'TB.'

'You're joking,' said Faure. 'Get him out quick. Go call the superintendent.'

It didn't take long. Moreau was led outside, away from everyone, back onto the central yard. How lovely, he thought, to breathe in the fresh air. It was a dull day, heavy clouds sweeping across the sky. Everything grey. With a jolt, he saw snaking towards him, a long line of children wearing their coats and hats, some with small cases or parcels, escorted by numerous guards. The main gates were open, a few policemen standing by. Were they going east, to Poland, as Mirabeau had said?

The superintendent arrived, a gaunt man with a pencil moustache. 'How long have you had it?' he barked.

'I s-saw my doctor last week.'

He eyed Moreau, squinting. 'Looks bad. You better not have passed it on. Why didn't you say anything?'

41

'I tried but no one listened.'

'Where's your star?' he asked, pointing at Moreau's coat.

'That's it, I'm not a Jew.'

'You're not? Your papers,' he said, snapping his fingers. The man took them, holding them gingerly, as if fearful of contracting the disease. 'Why, you really are not a Jew.'

'I tried to tell them that too.'

The man eyed him while Moreau held his handkerchief to his mouth. For good effect, he coughed.

The superintendent returned his papers. 'Get out of here. Faure, give him a few francs for the train fare.'

'Eh? Me?'

The superintendent walked off. Moreau stopped himself from thanking him. Reluctantly, Faure handed him the money.

'Thank you.'

He stood there, coughed again, unsure what to do.

'Well, what are you waiting for?' asked Faure. 'A taxi? The gates are open. Fuck off out of here.'

'Oh, right.' Moreau couldn't quite believe it could be that easy. Mirabeau had been right. 'Right, yes. Thank you.'

As he turned to leave, his heart hammering with delight, he heard the scream. '*Papa!*'

Shit, it was Marguerite. Turning he saw her amongst all those children, holding Lanky to her chest, its red and yellow vivid under the murky sky. 'Papa, Papa!'

'Oh my God,' he muttered. His daughter, his gorgeous daughter. 'Marguerite,' he called. Calling her name was a mistake. Marguerite, on hearing her father's voice, broke away from the pack and, still clutching Lanky, started running towards him, sidestepping a guard.

'Stop,' cried the guard.

'Papa.'

'Marguerite.'

'Halt.'

'Papa.'

A gunshot ran out.

His heart hammered. 'No, Marguerite, get back; for Christ's sake, get back.'

'Papa!' Still she ran towards him, her coat flapping open.

'Halt.'

'Stop, Marguerite.'

A second gunshot. She seemed to fly through the air before landing in a crumpled heap on the mud-packed ground, her fingers still gripping onto Lanky.

'Noooo! Marguerite, Marguerite, Margueriiiiite!'

*

The former postman seemed on the verge of fainting. 'Are you OK, Moreau?' asked Gustave Garnier, the former teacher, placing his hand on the man's shoulder.

43

'There was nothing I could do for them while I was there,' said Moreau, aware of all eyes on him. 'You have to believe me. If I escaped, I could have helped them. That was my idea; to help them.'

'I didn't know you'd been married before,' said Roger Béart, the older man. 'Or that you had another daughter.

'Yes. I've no idea what happened to Lily. I guess she perished, like so many others there.'

'Good god,' said Antoine Leclerc, the younger man.

The postman put his head in his hands. To think tonight, or was it lunchtime? he'd be seeing his daughter, the one he and Isabella, Madam Giono, had had just before the end of the war, and she'd be bringing his granddaughter. He loved them dearly, but now the prospect of seeing them chilled him.

The men eyed him for a while, feeling a mixture of contempt and pity. No man should see his child killed like that. No man.

Gustave Garnier, the former teacher, removed his glasses and polished them with a handkerchief. 'Would you like to hear my story now? If Henri can bare his soul, then I reckon it's time I did too.'

'If you're sure, Gustave,' said Leclerc.

'Yes, I am. I have to…'

The Teacher's Story

Gustave Garnier arrived at school early, as was his habit, to grab a cup of coffee before the kids arrived. The secondary school was quite the largest in the town; modern, recently built, with some three hundred pupils, it was the envy of educational establishments across the region. The reason for Garnier's early starts was that Mademoiselle Bouchez, the maths teacher, was another early bird. Garnier found Mademoiselle Bouchez terribly attractive in her pencil skirts, high-heeled shoes and her black-rimmed spectacles. Far too glamorous for a teacher. Each morning, they ran through the same routine – both making their coffees, his with milk and sugar, hers without, then he would sit and read the newspaper in the staffroom while she took hers to her classroom. So their only time together, much to Garnier's disappointment, lasted a matter of a couple of minutes. Garnier always hoped that she'd stay and talk. But she never did.

He knew the reason – six months before, long before the Germans had arrived (a lifetime ago), Garnier had asked her out. He'd planned it for weeks, waiting for a sign that his advances may be accepted. No sign came and, frustrated with waiting, he'd decided to force the issue and ask her right out. It'd been quite the hardest thing he'd ever done. This was when she still took her early morning coffee in the staffroom. They were quite alone. Only the headmaster was around and he was, as usual, ensconced in his office. It was a Wednesday. He had planned to ask her Monday but lost his nerve, ditto Tuesday. In the end, he went for it with a 'what's the worst that can happen' attitude.

'Mademoiselle Bouchez, have you seen that new film by Jean Renoir – what's it called? Rules of the Game, that's it. Rules of the Game. It's meant to be very good, so I'm told. I wondered if… I mean, if–'

She looked at him through her spectacles as if he'd just run over her cat. 'Yes?' she asked nervously.

'Well, whether you'd… we could go together; to the cinema, I mean.'

'Oh, erm. It's kind of you, Monsieur Garnier, but I'd…'

'No, of course. I understand. Oh, look, here's Paul.' Never had he been so pleased to see Paul Dauphin, the art teacher, with his multi-coloured cardigan and arty, unkempt hair. 'Hello, Dauphin,' he said gushingly, causing Dauphin to raise his eyebrows in surprise. 'Have you seen Rules of the Game?'

'Yes, it's meant to be shit.'

Despite herself, Bouchez laughed.

'What's so funny?'

'It's nothing,' she said, shooting Garnier a furtive look.

*

A week later, Dauphin buttonholed Garnier in the gents' toilet. 'Hey, Garnier, you were right about that film,' he said, standing at the urinal.

'Film?' asked Garnier, washing his hands.

'The Rules of the Game, it's very good.'

'You saw it?' He looked at his reflection in the mirror.

'I was told it was rubbish, but it's excellent. Nora Gregor is great in it.'

'That's good.'

'Yeah, and guess what? Mademoiselle Bouchez enjoyed it too.'

*

That was all of six months ago. It was now July 1940. The Battle of France was over – the nation had fallen and surrendered to the triumphant, swaggering Germans. The future had never seemed so uncertain.

The end of the school term was fast approaching – only a

47

couple of weeks to go. Half past eight – the school kids piled into their classrooms; the German occupation had done nothing to dampen their boisterousness.

Garnier, literature teacher, pushed his glasses up his nose and waited for his charges to settle down. He knew he was a popular teacher but could never work out whether it was because the children actually liked him or simply because they found him a bit of a pushover. The classroom was large, overlooking the school entrance. The morning sun shone through the window catching dust motes thrown up by the movement of pupils and chairs. Along the side wall was a map of the world plus several portraits of famous writers from down the ages – Victor Hugo, Voltaire, Jules Verne and others. In the corner, near the door, a display of poems his pupils had written under the theme, 'Reflections'. The poems were, almost without exception, fairly atrocious. But for this, he couldn't blame them. The kids may still have been boisterous, but the war and the arrival of the enemy had unnerved them, and himself, to varying degrees. A couple of them had lost family members – fathers, brothers or cousins, killed or taken prisoner. These were not the easiest of times. The illustrations many had added were, by and large, of much better quality. Paul Dauphin, the art teacher, damn him, was bloody good at his job. He could make an artist out of a blind man.

'So, I trust you all managed to memorise a sonnet. Michel, remind the class, if you'd be so kind, what constitutes a sonnet?'

Michel, one of Garnier's keenest students, did as told with, thought Garnier, perhaps a little too much elaboration.

Mid-morning, the children had their break. Monsieur Pérec, the head, called a meeting, allowing his staff three minutes to get their coffees. The staffroom, akin to a waiting room filled with armchairs, was full. Its walls were decorated with several of Monsieur Pérec's notices that no one ever read. The aroma of sweat and fresh coffee wafted across the room. The shops were fast running out of real coffee so people savoured every sip, thinking it might be the last. Every teacher crammed in. Given the lack of chairs, most had to stand, and Garnier had arrived early in order to claim one. Like an actor making his entrance, Monsieur Pérec made his appearance. Clearing his throat, he glanced round his audience. 'I've had a visit,' he announced without preamble. A bald-headed man with looming eyes behind large round spectacles, Pérec had been the school head since its opening a few years back. He wore his usual light brown suit, with the corner of a white handkerchief poking out of his breast pocket. Folding his arms, he continued, 'A small delegation of Germans came to see me this morning.'

A wave of titters and murmurs arose. 'I hope you showed

them the door,' said Paul Dauphin, putting his hand up.

'No, Dauphin, I did not. The fact is… It's very warm in here,' he said, wiping his shiny head with his handkerchief. 'Mademoiselle Bouchez, would you mind opening the window?'

Removing her glasses, Bouchez said, 'Are you asking me because I'm a woman?'

'No, Mademoiselle Bouchez, I'm asking you because you're closest to the window.'

With a sigh, Bouchez opened the window, teetering in her high heels, while Pérec tried to rearrange his handkerchief neatly into his breast pocket. Garnier tried to distract himself from staring at Bouchez's arse. Dauphin, sitting next to him, nudged him in the ribs, wagging his finger at him.

'Thank you,' said Pérec, stuffing the handkerchief into his trouser pocket. 'Where was I?'

'Our German friends,' said Monsieur Jobert, the chemistry teacher, fanning himself with a leaflet, a young man with a large moustache who lived life with a perpetual sweat.

'Ah, yes. They were in fact rather pleasant.' More murmuring. 'All right, calm down, calm down, everyone.'

'Absolutely,' said Jobert. 'Best thing that's happened to our nation. We need a bit of discipline.'

Dauphin, shaking his head, muttered, 'He's made a pact with Satan.'

'What was that, Monsieur Dauphin?' asked Pérec.

'I was just saying, Headmaster, that you can't always hate 'em.'

Bouchez giggled.

'Yes, well.' Adjusting his glasses, Pérec continued. 'The fact is that there are certain school texts that our new masters disapprove of.' Reaching for a pile of papers on the table behind him, he said, 'They seem most particular about this, and it affects most of you.'

'Even chemistry?' asked Jobert.

'And maths?' added Bouchez.

'Well, maybe not the sciences or maths. You are to take these lists for your subject, and ensure your classrooms are free of these texts.'

'You're joking, right?' said Dauphin.

'Do I look like a comedian?' said Pérec.

'Makes sense to me,' said Jobert, looking hotter by the minute.

'You would say that,' said Dauphin. 'You're half German, aren't you?'

'That I am and proud of it.'

'Which half? The German half or the idiot half?'

'What about the compilations and anthologies, Headmaster?' asked Garnier.

'Use your common sense, Garnier. Rip out the offending

pages but leave the rest intact. Right, that is all. Get your pupils to do the work but make sure it's done by the end of the day.'

Garnier returned to his classroom in time for the next class, scanning the list of authors who, for one reason or another, had to be removed from his bookshelves. On Pérec's suggestion, he got his pupils to find the books and pile them up on his desk at the front of the class. Garnier marked them off – 'Hemingway, Karl Marx, André Gide, Victor Hugo.'

'What's wrong with Hugo?' asked Michel.

'I don't know, Michel.'

'The bells, the bells,' said another, adopting a stoop in an attempt to impersonate Quasimodo.

'Yes, thank you, Jean. Now, let's get to the anthologies.'

'So, you really want us to rip out the pages, sir?'

'That's right, Yvonne. As simple as that.'

'Doesn't seem right to me.'

'Ours is not to reason.'

And so the class set to. Half an hour later, the wastepaper bin was full of discarded books and pages. Yvonne shook her head. 'How dare they?' she said.

'Ours is not to reason, Yvonne.'

'You said that already, sir.'

At the end of the school day, Garnier bumped into Dauphin and Bouchez in the staffroom. 'Well, did you do it?' asked Bouchez, gathering her things.

'No, I bloody didn't,' said Dauphin, buttoning up his cardigan.

'Oh, Paul,' said Bouchez, pulling on a strand of hair. 'I'm impressed.'

Pursing his lips, Dauphin smiled. 'One does what one can, Claire. We must show these people we're not going to roll over every time they click their fingers.'

'Indeed. I never realised you were so…'

'Yes?'

'Oh, I don't know, so… so strong, I guess.'

'My name, Mademoiselle B, is Spartacus.'

She laughed.

They seemed to have forgotten his presence, thought Garnier, hoping to slip away unnoticed. But, just as he'd reached the door, he heard Bouchez ask, 'What about you, Monsieur Garnier?'

'Me? What?'

'Did you refuse?'

'Refuse what?'

'Refuse to defile our culture, that's what,' said Dauphin, slinging his haversack over his shoulder.

'Well, no, I mean, it was an order, wasn't it? I mean… the headmaster said.'

Garnier found himself holding the door open as Dauphin and Bouchez sidled past him. Shaking his head, Dauphin tutted at him, while Bouchez, looking at him over her spectacles, mouthed the words 'Shame on you.'

Feeling thoroughly disgruntled, his briefcase in hand, Garnier was pleased to be heading home, but before he could make good his escape, halfway down the corridor, Pérec called him back. Lurking behind him was Monsieur Jobert, the corridor too narrow to accommodate both of them side by side.

'He hasn't done it, you know,' said the head, waving a sheet of paper in the air.

'I'm sorry?'

'That fool Dauphin. He hasn't gone through his books and now he's buggered off home.'

'I'd have him shot,' said the chemistry teacher, the sweat shining on his forehead.

'Yes, thank you, Jobert. You'll have to do it,' said Pérec, slamming Dauphin's sheet against Garnier's chest.

'Hey, what? That's not fair.'

Jobert laughed.

'You may spend all day with your students, Garnier,' said the head, 'but you don't have to talk like one of them. If the colonel comes back tomorrow morning and finds all these books by degenerate artists, as he called them, we're in trouble. Now if you'd be so kind…'

'He sure would appreciate it,' added Jobert, standing on his

54

tiptoes behind the headmaster.

'Jobert,' said Pérec, spinning round, 'have you not got anything better to do than follow me around all day?'

'But I wanted to get home,' said Garnier.

'Your home will still be there when you return, Monsieur Garnier. We don't work to a timesheet when it comes to the Germans, so get to it, if you please.'

Monsieur Dauphin's classroom was as chaotic as any art teacher's, examples of his pupil's work on every available inch of wall. Glancing at them, Garnier had to twist his head this way and that just to try and understand half of them. Some of it, most of it, was eye-poppingly explicit – flesh, so much flesh – writhing, pulsating, naked flesh; phalluses, flowers all open, red and inviting like… like… If this wasn't degenerate art, he didn't know what was. What was Dauphin trying to teach these kids? He felt embarrassed even to stand within this small temple of teenage artistic wantonness. In a cupboard behind the desk, he found the books – dozens and dozens of them. This, he thought, could take a while. There goes his evening of doing nothing. George Grosz, Wassily Kandinsky, Paul Klee, Marc Chagall, Max Ernst. God, he hadn't heard of any of these artists but, flipping through the pages, he could see why the Germans wanted them banned. You can't show impressionable youth stuff like this. Show them stuff like this and they end up… oh, they already had, thought Garnier, looking back at the artwork adorning the classroom walls. Dauphin was singlehandedly attempting to corrupt France's youth. It takes bloody foreigners to mend our ways.

Galvanised by irritation, Garnier took a pair of scissors and a utility knife from Dauphin's pot of materials and set to work – cutting here, slashing there, hacking at degeneracy, pornography, all this filth dressed up as art.

'You can't fool me, Dauphin, nor the Germans. "Oh, Monsieur Dauphin, I'm so impressed,"' he sang, pretending to suck on his hair, coiling invisible strands of it around his finger. '"You're so strong." "My name, Mademoiselle B, is Spartacus,"' he said, adopting a deep voice. '"I am Spartacus. I am Spartacus,"' he said, thumping his chest. 'Ha, I'll stuff a crown of thorns up your arse, then we'll see if you're Spartacus, you prick.'

'Is everything OK in here, Garnier?'

'Oh, good God, I'm sorry? Yes, thank you, Headmaster, everything's fine,' he said, slipping on a discarded book open on the floor. 'Whoa, I almost fell. Sorry, Headmaster. Just finishing.'

'I didn't mean you to make such a mess. Looks like you've had a bunch of kindergarten kids in here.'

'Ha-ha, yes.'

'It wasn't meant to be funny, Garnier.'

'No, sir, you're not a comedian.'

'Don't play the smart alec with me. Now, get on with it and clear all this up, would you?'

'Yes, of course, Headmaster.'

In clearing up, he threw all the discarded pages in the bin.

*

'Was it you?' bellowed Dauphin, charging into the staffroom the following morning.

'What's that?' asked Garnier, his face redder than the sky at night.

'It bloody was. You pig, you traitor, you… you…'

Garnier had expected nothing less – Dauphin was beside himself with rage. He'd been to his classroom a few minutes before school was due to start while Garnier waited in the staffroom, sipping his coffee, pretending to read the newspaper, waiting with increasing nervousness for the explosion of anger once the art teacher realised. It didn't take long. He heard Dauphin's footsteps pounding up the corridor. Unfortunately, Bouchez chose that moment to return to the staffroom, tottering in on her high-heeled shoes, and so saw Garnier's moment of humiliation.

'What on earth's wrong, Paul, love?' she asked.

Love? thought Garnier, she calls him 'love'?

'This… this…' he stuttered, pointing at Garnier hunched up in the armchair in the corner, trying to hide behind the newspaper. 'He's cut out pages from my textbooks.'

'Oh no,' said Bouchez, casting Garnier a withering look of contempt and disappointment. 'How could you, Monsieur Garnier?'

'I… I had no choice; Headmaster made me do it.'

'Headmaster made me do it,' said Dauphin, mimicking Garnier's weedy voice. 'You'd jump in a fire if he asked you to.'

Dauphin came over to Garnier. Garnier shrunk back, fearing he was about to be hit. Leaning over him, his hands on the chair's armrests, Dauphin whispered into his face, 'One day, once we've got rid of the Krauts and the day of reckoning comes, you, you turncoat, you quisling, you'll be the first against the wall. At least Jobert is open about his love for the Boche, but you're like a little slithering snake in the grass.'

*

A few months later, on the morning of 22 October 1940, the kids came to school in a state of high excitement. The evening before, many of them had listened to the radio as Winston Churchill relayed a speech in French to France from London. 'What did he say? What did he say?' asked the ones who'd missed it.

'He was funny,' said Michel. 'He said the Brits were waiting for the Boche invasion, and he said, "So are the fishes" in a

58

funny accent.'

'He sounded like my granddad,' said Yvonne.

The staffroom during morning break also talked about it.

'Me and Perrier have got an idea,' said Dauphin, pouring his ersatz coffee. Real coffee was now but a luxury available only to those who could afford it. 'We're going to join forces and do an exhibition and a play, a short one, mind you, and we're going to call it So are the fishes.'

'What a good idea,' said Bouchez, polishing her spectacles. Garnier had noticed – whenever she spoke to Dauphin, she wore the same silly, soppy expression. Nauseating. He knew they were dating but were trying to keep it a secret. Monsieur Pérec wouldn't approve.

'Sure is, Mademoiselle B,' he said with a wink.

'You are clever.'

'I think you should be careful,' said Jobert. 'Whatever that drunkard Churchill says, it'll soon be the Brits' turn. The Germans will ring their necks like so many chickens, you mark my words.'

'You would say that, you half Kraut,' said Dauphin, settling in his chair. 'I can never get used to this coffee; it's disgusting. What do you think, eh, Garnier?'

'Me? I don't drink the stuff.'

'No, I mean will the Germans invade Britain?'

'I don't know,' he said, quietly.

'No, you wouldn't.'

'Does the head know about your little project?' asked Jobert.

'I haven't told him yet.'

'He won't like it.'

'He will when I tell him.'

But Dauphin never did tell the headmaster. Instead, he launched straight into the project. It certainly galvanised the kids but it took up all his time – Monsieur Perrier, the drama teacher, had taken ill, so the whole endeavour fell on Dauphin's shoulders. He got his class to write up a ten-minute play while others began work on producing paintings around the theme of Churchill's speech.

One Friday morning, on his way to class, Garnier popped into the school office to collect his post from his pigeonhole. He found the school secretary at her desk, typing, laughing to herself. 'Morning, Mademoiselle Artaud,' he said cheerfully. 'Something's amusing you.'

'Oh, Monsieur Garnier, good morning to you. It's this play that Monsieur Dauphin's class have written. I'm just typing it up. It's so funny.'

'Is it?' asked Garnier, grumpily.

That same morning, Monsieur Pérec finally caught wind of Dauphin's project and immediately brought it all to an end. In a typed memo circulated to all staff, he said it wasn't for teachers to exploit the children into provoking the German authorities.

Dauphin took it quite well, thought Garnier. He drank his usual ersatz coffee in silence, reading a newspaper. He didn't speak and no one, not even Bouchez, spoke to him.

That afternoon, about to go home, Garnier returned to the office. The place was deserted; he could hear Mademoiselle Artaud's voice coming from the headmaster's office. Finding nothing new in his pigeonhole, Garnier noticed the typewritten play on her desk. Picking it up, he saw two carbon copies. Before he had time to think about it, he swiped the bottom copy and, folding it into two, quickly stuffed it into his jacket pocket.

That evening, back at home with his cat lying on his lap, he read the play. 'So Are the Fishes, a play in one act,' he read aloud. Consisting of just one side of foolscap, he read it quickly. 'It's not funny at all,' he said on finishing it. 'You could do better, Mimi,' he added, stroking his cat. 'You are clever, Paul,' he said, mimicking Mademoiselle Bouchez's voice. 'So bloody clever.'

It was only as he was going to bed that the idea came to him. Grinning at himself in the bathroom mirror, he said, 'Yes, that's it. That's it! I'll show you, you clever, smug bastard.'

For once, he went to bed happy.

*

A week later, a delegation of Germans arrived at the school in a convoy of three cars.

'The Boche are here,' said Yvonne in a high-pitched voice, halfway through Garnier's effort to instil in his pupils an appreciation of French nineteenth-century poetry.

Immediately, the whole class rose as one from their seats and rushed over to the windows. 'Sit down,' shouted Garnier in a futile attempt at maintaining order.

'Look at that car,' said a bespectacled boy called Henri. 'Citroën Eleven CV. Beautiful.' 'Why are they here?' asked Michel. 'Perhaps they've come to arrest the headmaster.' 'There're enough of them.' 'That one's got an eye patch.' 'Yeah, he looks like a pirate.'

Unable to resist it, Garnier joined them at the window. A few soldiers hung around the vehicles, one of them pulling the creases out of a pennant, while a colonel wearing a greatcoat, accompanied by a couple of privates, approached the main school entrance.

The bell signalling the end of class rang. 'OK, you may gather your things and leave in an orderly fashion. *I said* in an orderly fashion. Tomorrow we will be continuing...' By the time he'd come to the end of the sentence, every child had gone, a loud, chaotic exodus of overexcited school kids. The classroom door swung shut, a piece of paper floated to the ground, the air settled. '… by looking at the poetry of Paul Verlaine,' said Garnier quietly.

Garnier quickly made his way to the staffroom. The school was abuzz with news of the Germans' arrival.

'The colonel's talking to the headmaster,' said Jobert, the sweat pouring off him. 'In his office – with the door closed,' he emphasised.

'What do you think they want?' asked Bouchez, brushing her hair, her head tilted to one side.

'How should I know?'

Various teachers came and went. Dauphin came in, almost staggering, as if he'd just survived a stampede. 'Bloody kids have gone feral,' he said, catching his breath.

Bouchez went up to him. Laying her hand on his chest, she said, 'You all right, Paul?'

'Yeah, sure I am.'

More teachers came in, all as excitable as the children, speculating on the German presence within the school, laughing nervously. The place soon filled up. Jobert looked down the corridor. Barely able to contain himself, he announced, 'They're coming. The headmaster and the colonel.'

Conversations stopped short mid-sentence; a sudden silence descended; everyone stood still as the door swung open. 'This way, Colonel,' said Monsieur Pérec.

The colonel stepped into the room, a fair-haired man with a bright red face as if his collar was too tight and his stomach overhanging his belt. Jobert, Garnier noticed, stood straight, his chin up, looking as if he might salute any moment.

Pérec hopped around behind the colonel, his usual confidence absent. 'This is our staffroom,' he said, quietly, aware of all eyes upon him. 'It's a bit small for all the staff we have.'

The colonel, not responding, said, 'Well?'

'Yes, of course, erm…' Scanning everyone, he caught Dauphin's eye. 'Paul, erm…'

'Are you Paul Dauphin?' asked the colonel.

'What of it?'

'I have to ask you to come with me.'

It was only then that Garnier noticed the presence of the German privates outside the staffroom door and, behind them, a number of schoolchildren trying to see around them.

'Why?'

'It is best you come with me.'

Bouchez sidled up to him, looping her arm through Dauphin's. Pérec raised his eyebrows. Her presence emboldened the art teacher. 'Not until you tell me why.'

The colonel considered him for a moment as if weighing up his opponent. 'Have it your way.' Retrieving a sheet of paper from his inside pocket, he said, 'This has come to my attention.'

Even from afar, Garnier recognised the sheet of paper straight away. 'This is what I wanted,' he thought to himself. So why, he wondered, did he feel so sick?

'What children wrote this? One child or more?'

Dauphin didn't hesitate. 'None of them,' he said firmly. 'I wrote it all myself. Good, isn't it?' More schoolchildren had converged outside the staffroom, the ones behind standing on tiptoe.

'None of the children had any part in writing this silly play?'

'If it's so silly, why are you so worried about it?'

The colonel clicked his fingers. Immediately, the two soldiers appeared, the kids directly behind them almost falling through the door. 'Take him,' said the colonel.

'No,' screeched Bouchez.

One of the soldiers pushed her aside. Dauphin put up no resistance as the two men grabbed an arm each. 'Hey, hey, steady; mind the cardigan.'

'Leave him be,' said Bouchez.

'It's OK, Mademoiselle B. I'll be back soon; you'll see. Spartacus, remember?' he said with a wink. Shaking his arms free of the soldiers, he told them he'd go willingly. The colonel nodded his consent.

Garnier didn't know who'd started it but suddenly everyone was clapping. He joined in, had to, he thought. Only Pérec and

Jobert refrained, their faces reddening. And the applause got louder as the two soldiers escorted Dauphin out of the staffroom. The children at the door stood aside. They had also begun applauding. Starting with Mademoiselle Bouchez, the teachers, including Garnier, followed them out, still clapping while, in turn, the kids followed them. Dauphin's ovation got louder as more and more children joined the procession, following the teacher and his escorts down the corridor, past the offices and outside onto the school drive.

Outside, the clouds hung heavy, the atmosphere dank, the branches of distant trees swayed in the wind. On seeing the mass of staff and students coming towards them, the soldiers leaning on the cars stood. One ground a cigarette into the gravel. At their prompting, Dauphin headed for the second car. On reaching it, he turned to face his audience. Smiling, he bowed and waved. Bouchez with tears in her eyes clapped even louder. Garnier felt dizzy, the ground in front of him going in and out of focus. I'm Spartacus, he thought; I'm Spartacus. Last out of the school came the colonel and the headmaster, followed by Jobert. The colonel and the headmaster shook hands. Garnier noticed the headmaster surreptitiously wipe his hand on the back of his trousers. Jobert pulled a face. Approaching the car in front, the colonel nodded at his men. The back door of the second car opened and Dauphin, with a final wave, was bundled in.

And still, the clapping continued. Bouchez, with tears streaming down her face, began singing: 'Arise, children of the Fatherland, The day of glory has arrived.' On hearing the familiar tune, the children nearest her joined in. 'Against us, tyranny raises its bloody banner. Do you hear, in the countryside?' One by one, they all joined in. Soon, the whole drive reverberated to the sound of singing, the voices becoming bolder with each line. 'To arms, citizens, Form your battalions, Let's march, let's march!' The colonel gazed at them all, shaking his head as if in disbelief. With his adjutant holding open the car door, the colonel climbed in.

Still singing, the children and teachers watched as the three cars started up and leisurely drove down the drive, through the gate with its granite gate posts, and out and away. 'Let the impure blood water our furrows.' And then came the silence. Monsieur Pérec didn't need to say it; the children turned and slowly traipsed back indoors, back to class. Rooted to the spot and with the tune of La Marseillaise still ringing in his ears, Garnier watched them all leave, one by one, followed by the teachers. No one spoke. But everyone could feel it – the solidarity, the strength in the silence, the determination in their hearts. Garnier knew then, at that moment, that one day, maybe many years in the future, but one day, the French would prevail, and France would be France once again. History would prove the Dauphins of this world right. And with it came the realisation that he'd never be able to look at himself in the mirror again. His Pyrrhic victory brought no pleasure. His own sense of shame made him wince.

Turning around, he realised that Bouchez had been standing right behind him. 'Oh, Mademoiselle Bouchez, I'm…' He didn't know what to say. Her eyes bored into his, penetrating his very being. He wanted to lie, to say it was Jobert's fault, that Jobert had sent them the transcript of the play, Jobert the collaborator. But there was no point; she knew. He could see it in her eyes – she knew. Suddenly, she threw her head back and spat at him. He stood stock-still, feeling her spittle dribble down his cheek. Pushing past him, she walked back into the school, her high heels crunching in the gravel. It was only as he heard the door slam shut, he realised he was crying.

*

'Phew, so you let a man get arrested out of nothing more than petty jealousy,' said Roger Béart, the former soldier. 'What happened to him?'

'They let him out of course,' said Garnier, trying to sound upbeat about it. 'So, it was no big deal, you see? And then he married Mademoiselle Bouchez. So, you see… all's well that ends well,' he said, removing his glasses and rubbing his eyes.

'And was that it?' asked Henri Moreau, the former postman.

'Yes, absolutely. Well, OK, maybe not…'

'You need to tell us, Gustave,' said Antoine Leclerc.

Garnier sighed. 'OK, I've come this far, I might as well tell you. One day a few weeks later, a German soldier was shot and killed in the street. Monsieur Dauphin was one of those they shot in reprisal. Once he'd been arrested, the Germans had his card marked. So, when they came looking for people to execute, they came knocking at his door.'

'So,' said Roger Béart. 'It's fair to say that if it hadn't been for your treachery, Monsieur Dauphin would still be with us.'

'That's a bit unfair–'

'Actions have consequences,' said Leclerc. 'We all know that. And we're all guilty of it, Garnier. You're not alone.'

'He's right,' said Béart. 'My story's hardly any better. Do you want to hear it?'

The Soldier's Story

1917

They'd been riding for days. A battalion of French cavalry, traipsing through the Palestinian desert. The officers knew where they were heading, another camp some eighty kilometres away, but hadn't seen fit to tell the men. Not that it'd make much difference anyway – no one knew one destination from another in this godforsaken place. To Private Roger Béart and his khaki-clad comrades, it was all the same, just mile upon mile of desert and sun. He was tired, dead tired, as were all the men, as were the horses and the mules. The monotonous landscape did little to raise their spirits – valleys of sand surrounded by mountains of sand. By day, the men rode their horses, sweltering under the scorching heat, only their wide-brimmed straw hats saving them from the worst. The mules brought up the rear laden with the precious water tanks, one of them pulling the wagon containing the Lewis gun. Water rations were strictly controlled – they had plenty of water but it had to last, and one always had to have enough for contingencies. And then there was the sand, the bloody sand. It got everywhere – in their food, their water, in their mouths, their eyes, under their clothes. Jesus, thought Béart, even when you went for a piss, you'd find sand on your cock. Their whole world had been reduced to nothing but sand and sun, both unrelenting, both tortuous.

By night they shivered from the cold. Those lucky enough not to be on guard duty lay on their backs under their blankets gazing up at the limitless glittering night sky, the multitude of stars brighter than they'd ever seen, the moon close enough to touch. Many found the sky at night comforting, putting into perspective man's petty squabbles, but Béart hated it – its vastness frightened him, made him conscious of his mortality.

Béart and his horse, Hector, named, he'd been told, after Berlioz, the composer, had been partners for over two years. They'd got to know each other; he knew Hector's moods, his little foibles. And Béart loved him in a way he'd never loved anyone else. Hector was a gelding, fifteen hands tall, dark brown in colour, almost red, like a red setter, a blaze of white on his nose and one white sock. No question about it, he was a handsome devil. But this war and this unending trek had begun to take its toll on Hector. He was nine years old – too old for this sort of thing, thought Béart. He deserved to be retired off; he'd done his bit for France. His coat was not as shiny as before, he hung his head too low. Man and beast — united in their sufferance.

It was the fifth day. Each day Major Brunet sent a couple of men off in advance to scout for enemy movement. Meanwhile, Béart was fuming. He'd lost half a packet of cigarettes. Some bastard had nicked them during the night. Riding alongside Moulin, he asked, 'Who'd do that to his fellow comrade?'

'One mean bugger, that's who.'

'I'd rationed them all out — four in my pocket for the day, the rest of the pack in me haversack. Now, I've got four left to last God knows how long.' He could tell that Moulin wasn't that bothered about his misfortune. He didn't mention it again. Everything about this place was a misfortune, and there was always that fear of an ambush, of being caught unawares. Bloody slippery fellows, those Turks. Béart's missing cigarettes were not likely to feature highly on Moulin's list of concerns. Moulin's face had blackened from the sun and ingrained dirt, and was lined with dried streaks of sweat. His eyes looked vacant; he'd aged twenty years in five days. He'd already grown a beard which he scratched and pulled upon constantly; his clothes were wet from sweat, his palms calloused from holding the reins for so many hours a day. But every man was Moulin; every man looked the same. And Moulin, like everyone else, rarely spoke. Talking required too much effort. Instead, each man fell into his own thoughts, the things that gave him comfort, that reminded him of home. Béart daydreamed about rain. Never again would he complain about rain. He dreamt of cold winter nights at home in Normandy, sitting beside the fire, a dog at his feet, while his mother knitted or, occasionally, played a simple tune on the piano. Then to bed with a hot brick warming the icy cold sheets, snuggling down for the night, the clock ticking on the bedside table.

Béart had been brought up with horses. His mother said he knew how to ride before he could walk. They lived on a farm. His father worked hard, up at dawn, working until late in the evening. One night he didn't come home. His mother searched the outbuildings, calling his name, but couldn't find him. A sleepless night ensued. A labourer found him the following morning – lying face down in a field. Dead. A heart attack. Not yet fifty. No age. Béart was still too young to take the farm over, for which he was thankful – there was no way he wanted to be a farmer. So his mother sold the farm and lived in moderate comfort in the town. She never said so but Béart always suspected that she was happier in town, away from the unrelenting harshness of the countryside. Béart didn't miss it either, but he did miss the horses. As soon as he was old enough, he got a job as a stable hand and horses were once again at the centre of his life. In the summer of 1915, he was conscripted. The army, seeing his equine affinity, put him in the cavalry. His mother was delighted. Her son looked so handsome in his uniform. Pity he lacked the education to be an officer, but that was hardly his fault. He'd soon prove himself though; he'd soon be promoted.

Two years on, and Béart hadn't been promoted. Still the lowly private, the lowest of the low, still yet to fire his gun in anger, yet to see the whites of their eyes. But better a private in the cavalry, as he always said, than a non-commissioned officer in the infantry.

Béart stroked Hector's flank – he too was tired; he could see that. The men often walked, leading their horses by the reins, not only to give the horses a bit of a rest but also to allow the men to use a different set of muscles, and to ease the saddle sores.

Further to his right, Béart saw Private Sarde. 'Hey, Sardines,' he called out. 'Give us a tune.' Private Sarde, or Sardines, the 'toothless wonder', was in the habit of playing his mouth organ – a couple of ditties every hour or so. Never failed to lift a man.

Sarde shook his head. 'Can't,' he said, running his fingers across his lips. His lips were cracked – everyone's lips were cracked. Poor old Sarde, poor old everyone; no more mouth organ.

It was the sixth day, about ten in the morning, the men were on the move, the sun was already high in the sky, sapping the men of their strength. Their breakfast of bully beef, biscuits and black tea already seemed an eternity ago. The two men sent out to reconnoitre came cantering back, only half an hour after leaving. Major Brunet, on seeing them approach, put his hand up, bringing the whole company to a halt.

'Whoa there, Hector,' said Béart.

'Oi, oi,' said Moulin. 'Something's up. An ill wind brings them back in a hurry.'

The corporal, his face beneath his hat red with exertion and excitement, reported back to the major. Major Brunet, standing in his stirrups, listened, dismissed the corporal, then, dismounting, called in his officers. Maps were produced, compasses consulted, plans scribbled on paper.

'This could be juicy,' said Moulin.

Even Sardines managed a quick burst on his mouth organ until a lieutenant cut him short. The officers needed to concentrate.

Ten minutes later, Major Brunet was ready to issue his orders. Every man had dismounted, holding their horses by the reins. Gathering around, they listened with keen interest. 'OK, men,' said the major, shielding his eyes, 'this is the situation. Three kilometres south of here is a small Turk outpost, about a hundred men. Because of the lay of the land, we can't avoid them. The hillocks on either side of the valley there are too difficult for the horses, let alone the mules. We have no choice but to face them head-on. "A" Platoon will split into two and on foot detour around the dunes, both east and west. From there, they will lead the attack. The rest of us will follow through. The gradient favours us. A three-pronged attack should do it quite easily. Any questions?'

There were no questions.

It didn't take long for "A" Platoon to get ready. Led by a lieutenant with long whiskers, off they went on foot, bayonets fixed, leaving puffs of sandy dust in their wake.

Galvanised, Béart and his colleagues got ready – a quick clean of their rifles, hats off, helmets on, a check on ammo, the tightening of their belts, a gulp of water, an extra biscuit. 'This is more like it,' said Moulin, grinning, easing his sabre in and out of its holster. 'They won't know what's hit 'em. Got a spare fag?'

'No,' snapped Béart.

Tightening Hector's girth, Béart remounted. Hector seemed to know. He was immediately alert, his ears pricked forward, stamping his hooves. 'Good boy,' said Béart, slapping his neck. Despite the intensity of the heat, Béart shivered. Putting his hand on his chest, he realised how fast his heart was beating. He knew what lay ahead would be a mere skirmish but going into battle upon his horse was what he'd trained for, and he felt both excited and frightened.

The men were ready, the horses geared up. A mule had been

packed with the Lewis gun. The major, mounted on his bay stallion, trotted up and down issuing his orders. 'On receiving "A" Platoon's signal, we shall move into place – the furthest we can go without being spotted. We'll move up the Lewis and let them have it. Then, on my signal, we'll charge. Main thing, men, is to fan out, don't group together. Rein your charges in until I give the command. Got it?'

Ten minutes later, the signal, via a mirror reflected in the sun, came flashing from the horizon. 'Right, let's go,' cried the major. 'March at ease, steady as she goes. No talking, no smoking.'

And so, one hundred cavalrymen set off. No sound except the clumping of the horses' hooves on the dry sand, the creaking of saddles and the champing of bits. Béart tried to muffle a cough as more sand lodged in the back of his throat.

The men followed the major two kilometres down the valley, the sun at its worst, boring into them. Behind them, the medical lads, their Red Cross brassards round their arms, their medical kits at the ready, banging against their saddles. Approaching a bend, the major put his hand in the air. The men pulled their horses to a stop. Major Brunet, having given the Lewis gunners the order to prepare, considered the situation through his field glasses, his lieutenants on either side of him. Peering through the heat rays, the outpost looked pathetically vulnerable, thought Béart – a few straw huts, sturdy-looking tents, strong enough to resist the desert sand, a Turkish flag limp without a breeze. Men in khaki, some in red fezzes and red sashes across their tunics, pottered about, and, rather incongruously, thought Béart, a couple sat in deck chairs as if at the seaside. A number of men with toasting forks congregated around a campfire, their rifles slung around their shoulders, the fire emitting wafts of black smoke. Others kept guard over a cannon. Béart almost pitied them – they had no idea.

And then it started – the two portions of "A" Platoon charged down the valley from opposite directions, their guns blazing. Hector snorted, pulling on his bit. Both man and horse were itching to charge, but the major held them back. The Lewis gunners did their work, the guns spewing five hundred rounds a minute. The Turks roused themselves immediately, manning their guns, firing back at "A" Platoon.

'Hold it, hold it,' shrieked the major. 'Sabres at the ready.'

The "A" Platoon men had breached the camp; hand-to-hand fighting ensued.

Major Brunet, with his sword poised in the air, keeps his nerve. 'Steady, steady...'

Hector prances on his feet.

With a whoosh, the major brings down his sword, its silver blade catching the sun. 'Chaaaarge!' he yells.

Reins are dropped, spurs dig into horses' flanks. The noise

is intense. Leaning forward in his saddle, Béart swings his sword. He screams, his heart pumps with adrenalin and elation. A memory flashes through his mind – galloping through the field at the back of the farm, a blustery autumn day, the wind in his hair, taking a gate at full speed, the joy of flying through the air. Hector, bless him, surviving these last few days on minimal rations, has lost none of his speed. The hooves of so many horses produce clouds of sand. The Turks fire on them, the whistling of bullets, the men meet a hail of lead head-on. Someone falls. A horse is hit, falling to the ground with a terrible yelp, his legs caught beneath him. Moulin, riding alongside, his helmet lopsided, is grinning, laughing. A shell whizzes overhead.

Approaching the camp, the men fan out, as the major had ordered. Béart sees a Turk, his rifle aimed right at him. The man fires. Instinctively, Béart ducks. Within a second, he's upon him, cutting him through with his sword. A spurt of blood, a scream, the deed is done in an instant. Béart pulls Hector up, swings him around, looking for someone else to kill. Men shout and curse, rifle fire pierces the air. Hector rears. Bringing him down, Béart catches the sight of Moulin falling from his horse. He sees a comrade bludgeon a Turk on the ground with his rifle butt. More gunfire. There are no Turks left standing.

The guns stop. The silence descends suddenly.

It's over too soon.

Béart, his every sense on full alert, brings Hector down to a trot. Men on prancing, snorting horses search for survivors, their swords at the ready. There's one there! He's injured, his shoulder a bloody mess but he cocks his revolver. Major Brunet leaps from his horse and finishes him off with his sword, the blade slicing through the man's chest. The man arches up as the revolver slips from his hand, then slumps. Using a rag, Brunet wipes the blood from his sword. Dismounting, the men look around for the rest of the wounded, following the sound of groaning and sobbing, and run each of them through with their swords. Screams come from every corner of the camp. Béart, having tied Hector's rein against a tent pole, is desperate to kill one more and is disappointed not to find one.

'I think that's it,' declares Major Brunet after a few minutes.

Surveying the scene, Béart views all the dead, so many of them, mostly Turkish. But there, amongst them, behind a ragged tent, is Moulin, a crimson hole in his forehead. Béart shakes his head. He wishes he'd given him that cigarette now. Going through his pockets, looking for something he might send home to his family, Béart finds his packet of cigarettes. 'You bastard,' he says, kicking the corpse in the ribs.

The air hangs heavy with smoke and dust and the smell of cordite. Horses snort. The tents, without exception, are torn to shreds, the straw huts burn, the black smoke drifting over the camp. Equipment and weapons lie scattered, a boot here, a fez there, a broken bayonet, pots and pans amongst the debris. Wounded French lie here and there, groaning. One of them screams, holding the bloody, congealed mess that is his thigh, his lower leg shot clean away. Another, his eyes dull, seems on the point of death. The first aid boys are already attending them.

It was then that Béart saw him. A Turk lying face down on the ground stirring into life. Rubbing the back of his head, he struggled up onto one knee, then the other. Béart, creeping up behind him, drew his sword. He was about to swing when the major shouted at him. 'Stop right there, Private.'

Béart lowered his sword.

Major Brunet approached the Turk, his revolver drawn. Béart held his breath, convinced the man was about to be shot. 'Get up,' said the major, gesturing with his revolver.

The Turk rose slowly to his feet, raising his hands. A tall man with jet-black hair, black, piercing eyes and a long, thin moustache, a scar on his cheek, he towered over the major. His tunic was badly torn, his face filthy, but beneath the dirt, Béart could see a young face, his eyes full of pride and hatred. The Turk said something, his voice assertive.

'Private, go call the lieutenants.'

Béart did as told. Stepping over a number of dead Turks, he

found one of the lieutenants with his revolver pressed against the temple of a stricken horse. Tears coursed down his cheeks as the man pulled the trigger. A couple of soldiers came running on hearing the sound of the shot. One of them, a sergeant, patted the lieutenant on the back. Béart allowed him a few seconds before approaching him. He found the second lieutenant with several men lifting buckets of water from a well. The whole camp, he realised, had been built around this well. The men were happy – the water was clean and fresh, and they could drink their fill and scrub their faces clean. Béart heard the familiar sound of the mouth organ – sitting on an upturned crate, Sardines winked at him.

Béart returned with the two lieutenants to find Major Brunet still with his revolver trained on his prisoner who stood upright, his back straight, his eyes cast far away. A few other soldiers stood nearby, rifles drawn. 'So, how many casualties did we sustain, Lieutenant?'

They both answered at once – 'Three dead, sir.' The taller one continued, 'Plus about a dozen wounded but only one seriously.'

'Does the wog speak French, sir?' asked the shorter lieutenant.

'No, he doesn't. Where's Ozen? He speaks Turkish.'

'Ah. He was one of the three.'

'Dead?'

'Sir.'

'Bloody nuisance.'

'Do you want us to kill him, sir?'

'What? This chap? Certainly not, Lieutenant. He's a captain. We've frisked him. Nothing on him apart from a photo and his ID papers. Captain Hakan Kazaz. We need to get him to intelligence.'

Béart noticed the man's photo lying face-up on the ground at his feet. The major had tossed it away. It was a shot of the man standing behind his seated wife. The woman's beauty caught him by surprise, the hint of Eastern promise, her exotic face, astonishing vibrant eyes – such beauty in this ugly, forgotten outpost.

'What about Dubas?' said the major. 'He speaks Turkish, doesn't he?'

'He only speaks Greek, sir.'

'Oi, Captain,' said the major to the Turk. 'Speak Greek? Or French?'

For a moment, Béart thought he saw the Turk shake his head but then realised he was just glancing between the three French officers in front of him.

'Damn it. I suppose we could just shoot him. We're certainly not taking him with us, far too much of a burden.' The major paced away, stopping in front of a Turkish corpse. Kicking the corpse, he returned. Lifting his revolver, he

84

pointed it at the Turk. The man cowered, knowing his end had come. But then, dropping his arm, the major said to his lieutenants, 'The man's a captain; he'll know stuff, potentially good stuff. We need a caged bird. And he'll talk. Look at him, he's a streak of piss.' Major Brunet spun round to face Béart. Béart stood tall. 'You, Private. What's your name?'

'Béart, sir. Private Roger Béart, number one, six–'

'Shut up.'

'Sir.'

Looking round at the other soldiers, he saw Sardines ambling by. 'Halt, you there, Private.'

'Who? Me, sir?' said Sardines in an exaggerated fashion, pointing at himself.

'Yes, you, sir. What's your name?'

'Jacques Sarde, sir.'

'What's happened to your teeth? Second thoughts, I don't want to know. Stand next to Péart there.'

'It's Béart, sir.'

'Right, you two – take this man back to base.'

Béart's face screwed up in confusion. 'Base, sir?' Did he mean the last place they'd stopped, or did he really mean… base?

'Yes, base. Just the two of you. Head due north: it shouldn't take you long. Take a horse each and put Captain Turk here on a mule. That should do it.'

'But… but, sir.'

The major approached him, his moustache twitching slightly under his nostrils. 'Yes?'

'It's… it's five days away.'

'So what? Once back in base, have a day off, then report for further duties. Understood?'

Shooting a glance at Sarde, Béart tried to compute what the major had told him.

'I said understood, private?'

'Y-yes, sir. Understood.'

'Get Sergeant Berri to kit you up with enough to keep both of you going for the duration. And him. Now listen, Private Péart…'

'It's Béart, sir.'

'Make sure Captain Turk arrives in one piece. It could be vital. Report to Brigadier Hallier, Intelligence Corps. Tell him I sent you. They'll know what to do with him. Right, off you go, private, report to Sergeant Berri. You too,' he added, turning to Sarde. As they left, Béart noticed Sarde step on the Turk's photo, whether by accident or design, he didn't know.

Half an hour later, Béart and Sarde and their respective horses were ready. They'd been given enough rations for man and horse for seven days, medical supplies, a couple of flares and spare ammunition. The mule was laden with water tanks, fresh from the well. They each had a map and a compass. All they had to do, they were told, was to retrace their steps and they'd soon find themselves back at base. Simple really.

Béart stroked Hector's muzzle and tickled him round the ears – something which always made Hector grin, exposing his teeth. Béart had always loved the smell of horse, that dry, earthy smell. It made him think of home, of his childhood; like a comfort blanket, it calmed him. The horse looked tired; he too had been through an ordeal. He'd loved a lot of horses over the years but perhaps none as much as Hector with his deep black eyes and his beautiful eyelashes. He loved his colouring, the white blaze and the one odd sock, as if he'd forgotten to put the other ones on.

With Captain Kazaz mounted on a mule, the three men headed off. It was mid-day. Béart half expected a farewell party, a shake of the hand from the major, a 'good luck and thank you'. There was nothing. They left as the medics saw to the wounded, as horses were patched up, and the men made use of the well.

'You got your mouth organ?' asked Béart.

'Course,' said Sarde, grinning, exposing his gums. 'Never go nowhere without it.'

'It's a long way to go.'

'So what? Everywhere's a long way.'

Fair point, thought Béart.

The men rode in silence. It was just too hot to talk. Captain

Kazaz kept his place in the middle while Béart brought up the rear. They walked for hour upon hour. The desert, Béart concluded, was a beautiful thing. Beautiful but threatening. A world without end, nature at its rawest, merciless.

Béart felt different somehow and it took him a while to work out why. He'd killed a man; driven his sword through his chest. Like losing one's virginity, it was something one could never undo. He was lucky, he supposed, that it had happened so quickly. He had no recollection of what the man looked like, only that he'd fired his rifle at Béart and so Béart felt no regret. What shocked him though was the degree of his bloodlust that followed, his desire to plunge his sword into another of them, to see Turkish blood upon its blade. He shivered at the thought of his depravity.

Several hours after setting off, as the sun settled, they decided to camp down for the night. They managed to find a boulder on a patch of barren grass. Not much but it'd do. Having fed, watered and rubbed down the horses and mule, they shared out their bully beef and biscuits and ate and drank in silence. By the time they'd finished, it was already pitch dark, night-time descending quickly. Béart lit the lanterns.

'It's not really fair, is it?' said Sarde, arranging the blankets.

'What's that?'

'Well, Captain Turk here gets a full night's sleep while the two of us have to make do with half each. Can't we just shoot him? Tell them he tried to run away, and we shot him. He probably knows sod all anyway.'

'Orders is orders, Sardine.'

'S'pose.'

Removing his helmet, Sardine stretched his legs, staring up at the night sky. After a while, despite his cracked lips, he began playing a tune on his mouth organ. With his rifle resting on his lap, Béart lit a cigarette and kept his eye on the Turk, the two men sitting cross-legged, face-to-face, staring at each other. 'Don't look so miserable, you bastard, you was lucky you weren't killed today,' he said to the Turk. 'Just think – you was the only one left alive. You're very young to be a captain.' The man had dark, piercing eyes that seemed to bore into him. He was, thought Béart, a good-looking bloke with his black hair and his pencil moustache, his pure, olive skin and his stubble. He wondered how he'd earned the scar. He thought about the woman in the photo, that dark beauty, her eyes, those eyes… 'Here,' he said, 'have a cigarette.'

The Turk looked at him as if suspecting a trick. Carefully, he reached out and took the cigarette and Béart's box of matches. Lighting the cigarette, he exhaled.

'No need to thank me,' said Béart, vaguely offended by the lack of acknowledgement. He realised he felt a little intimidated by this dark-skinned man with his black eyes and steely stare.

'Who are you talking to, Béart?' asked Sarde.

'Him, of course.'

'Captain Turk? You stupid bugger, you might as well talk to your horse.'

The following morning, the three men were up before dawn, breakfasted and ready. Time lost its meaning as the second and third days passed in a haze, merging into one.

On the fourth morning, having harnessed the horses and the mule, they set off just as the hazy sun began to show over the horizon, their shadows stretching before them. 'Still a long way to go,' muttered Béart.

'Bit windy today, ain't it?' said Sarde.

'It'll settle.'

But it didn't. At first, the sand blew around the horses' feet, steadily growing stronger. It was as if the desert was warning them, a warning unheeded by the two Frenchmen. On and on they trudged, hour after hour, the wind swirling around them, the horses having to pick up their feet. Béart pulled down his helmet and pulled his scarf up to cover his mouth but thought nothing of it. Captain Kazaz turned and said something to him, pointing to the horizon. Standing up in his stirrups, Béart couldn't work out what he was talking about. 'Hey, Sardine, Captain Turk's worried about something,' Béart shouted over.

'I'll give him something to worry about if he don't shut up,' came Sarde's response.

'Is it me or has it gone cold all of a sudden?'

'Bloody hell, you're right. Why's it gone so dark? Where's the bloody sun?'

Captain Kazaz shouted something at them, gesticulating.

'Christ, Sarde, he knows something.'

And then it hit them.

In an instant, their world turned yellow.

Seized by terror, Béart grappled with the reins, desperately trying not to fall off. The sand descended as if God Himself had thrown it in their faces. Screaming, the sand filled his mouth, despite the scarf, the sand blinding him. He had goggles in his pack but where was his pack? The world began spinning, faster and faster, all borders of normality erased, tossed as if he weighed nothing. The noise of the howling wind pummelled his ears; his every sense came under assault. Hector beneath him writhed and screamed. The intensity of it was unremitting. 'I can't breathe,' his mind screamed; 'I can't breathe.' The wind and sand flicked him off Hector like a bowling pin. He felt as if he was falling through space, unending and everlasting, no sense of direction. Utterly disorientated, he couldn't see, hear or feel anything, was only aware of the complete fear and his hopeless vulnerability. The sand whipped his face as if a million needles were pricking him all at once. 'It's going to bury me', he thought, his every fibre in panic; 'it's going to bury me.' Unable to tell whether he was upright or upside down, the wind blew him down, whipped him, pounded him. He wanted to lie in a foetal position, to close his eyes and make it go away but the fear of being buried alive stopped him.

How long it lasted, he had no idea – it could have been a minute, it could have been six hours. But then, suddenly, it stopped. Breathing manically, Béart tried to open his eyes, crying in pain as the minute granules of sand scrapped his eyeballs. On all fours, he coughed and spat and vomited out the sand, fearing lest he'd never be able to purge his insides of the stuff. Still dark, he looked around him, squinting, and realised with utter dread that nothing was the same. It looked like the surface of a faraway planet. Everything grey. He called out Sarde's name, Hector's, even Captain Kazaz. His voice echoed back to him, suspended on the calmer but still menacing wind. He put his hand on his head and realised that, despite the strap, his helmet had been whipped off. He reached for his pack but realised that that too had gone, as was his rifle. All that was left was his belt with its holster, his revolver inside. But nothing else. Then the fear seized him round the throat – he was as good as dead. No food, no water, no horse, no compass, nothing. Nothing in a world of nothing.

Standing up, his legs gave way. Grappling around on hands and knees, he cried out for help. It was then he heard it. With renewed strength, he got to his feet. 'Hector,' he yelled, his throat like sandpaper. 'Hector!' He could see the horse's silhouette. Lifting his feet through the sand, he stumbled towards his horse. Hector lifted his head as Béart fell against him, sobbing. And still attached to his quarters was Béart's pack containing his compass, food and a canister of water. The horse looked awful, his hair heavily matted, his eyes coated in sand. Pouring small amounts in his cupped hand, he offered the water to Hector who lapped it up, his tongue and the bristles on his muzzle rubbing against Béart's palm. He tried to remove the worst of the gunk out of his eyes. 'Good boy, good boy.' Hector's forage had gone with the mule. Scanning the horizon, he patted the horse. 'We're going to get out of this, Hector. God knows how but we will.'

The wind had finally died down, but the sky remained dark and a sand-filled mist settled over the dunes. He felt like the last man on earth. Consulting the compass, he started walking, leading Hector by the reins. 'This way's north,' he said, picking his way through the sand. 'Oh, shit, you're limping.' Patting the horse's flank, he said, 'Come on, boy, let's see what's wrong with you.' The white sock was bloodied; he'd cut himself; the gash was deep and ingrained with sand. He had no way of cleaning it – the medicine kit lost to the storm.

He heard a voice, a cry from somewhere. 'Who's that?' he cried. 'Sardine?' The figure came towards him, like a corpse rising from the earth, shrouded in mist. 'Is that you? Sardine?'

'*Merhaba*, hello.'

'Captain Turk, it's you.' Instinctively, he reached for his revolver, unclipping it from its holster.

'Where's your mule? Where's Private Sarde?'

The Turk spoke quickly, pointing vaguely in the distance.

'Where's your pack?'

The Turk mimicked drinking. Reluctantly, Béart allowed him a sip, no more. A rush of anger surged through him, taking him unawares; he hated the man with an intensity he'd never felt before. He realised he was going to have to share what little water he and Hector had with the bloody Turk; and in return, the Turk was able to offer nothing. All take, no give. He'd shoot the man; what did he care for saving him, for delivering him for the sake of information which would probably be out of date by the time they received it.

With his revolver, he gestured the way forward. 'Walk,' he said. 'Go on, walk.'

The Turk shot him a hateful look.

They walked and walked, how long, Béart didn't know, having no sense of time. Walking, walking, Kazaz in front, the sand sucking their feet, sapping their strength, only the sound of Hector chomping on his bit. They soon felt deadbeat. The Turk gestured, asking if he could ride the horse. 'No, you bastard, he's hurt his leg; he's in pain.'

Finally, Kazaz sank to his knees. Hector snorted, lifting his stockinged leg. 'I know, I know,' said Béart, stroking him. Captain Turk mimed eating and drinking. 'OK, we might as well have a stop.'

Sitting cross-legged, Béart passed the Turk a tin of bully beef from the pack, instructing him to open it. Little insects darted across the sand.

'Enough,' said Béart after the Turk had taken only a couple of mouthfuls. 'Come, pass it back.' Kazaz didn't look keen, tightening his grip around the tin. Béart cocked his revolver. Grudgingly, the Turk passed it back. Scooping out a handful, Béart got to his feet to feed Hector. The Turk screeched in protest.

Béart leapt on him, pushing him back. 'Back off, you bastard. I could quite happily kill you; so if you know what's good for you, butt out. You can starve to death for all I care but that horse – no, he ain't dying for you. Got it?'

Kazaz, his eyes infused with loathing, nodded.

Returning to Hector with the bully beef, he fed the horse. Hector looked exhausted, his eyes had lost their shine, his mouth full of saliva. 'I know it's meat, old boy, but you've got to eat something. Got to keep your strength up, eh? Yeah? Good boy. I'll fetch you some water. I'll get you back if it's the last thing I do. Just imagine, Hector, you're in a big field back at home. Green, lush grass, and trees round the sides, the sun shining, not like this, just a gentle sun and a few fluffy clouds.

Just you and a couple of ladies. Imagine, Hector, imagine that.'

Hector shook his head from left to right; he seemed to be imagining it.

Sitting back down, Kazaz and Béart eyed each other. He could see his hatred for the man reflected back in the Turk's eyes.

Night fell. Lighting a lantern, Béart sat back down opposite Kazaz, leaning on his pack, his revolver clamped in his hand. Eventually, the man fell asleep. Sarde's words came back to him, but now it was worse. The Turk could sleep but he, Béart, could not, knowing he couldn't afford to take his eyes off him for a second; convinced the man was capable of killing him with his bare hands.

How small he felt under the night sky looming above him in its infinity; how insignificant he felt surrounded by these mountains of sand, everywhere sand, sand, sand. Oh, to be home on the farm, playing in the fields, a hot, cooked meal waiting for him back in the warm kitchen, his mother in that rose-patterned apron, wooden spoon in her hand, greeting him with a kiss on his head. Oh, to be home… so far away, such a long time ago, home…

*

It was a chorus of little sounds that woke him up – the creak of Hector's saddle, a snort, the click of hoof against a stone, the jangle of a water can. Béart opened his eyes with a start – the sun was hovering just over the horizon. He was on his feet in an instant, his revolver still in his hand. 'Oi, stop, stop!'

Kazaz, digging his feet into Hector's sides, pushed the horse on.

'Stop! Stop or I'll fire.'

But he wasn't going to stop, Béart knew that. Lifting his arm, he aimed, squinting against the reddish sun. Trying to steady his shaking arm, he fired. And missed. He fired again, flustering, once, twice, thrice. Wild shots. The Turk whipped the horse with the reins, urging him on but Hector, who momentarily buckled, was in no hurry. Béart knew he had but one more chance. If he missed again, the Turk would be too far away. His life depended on this. Left eye closed, left hand steadying his right arm, he took aim. The shot rang out. Kazaz slumped. 'Yes!' He watched with a thumping heart as the Turk slid from the saddle, landing on the sand in a heap.

Leaving behind his pack, running over as best as he could, Béart found Kazaz breathing, still alive. Hector had come to a halt a few feet away, panting, struggling.

Kazaz, on his back, looked up at Béart's revolver pointing at him, a thin line of blood seeping from his mouth. The image of the man's exotic wife swept through Béart's mind. Too young to be a widow.

'Please… shoot me,' said the Turk between breaths.

'You… you speak French?'

'Yes, I speak French.'

'You speak French.' Of course, he remembered the Turk's reaction when surrounded by the major and the lieutenants. 'You mean, we didn't have to do this. If the major had known… We wouldn't be here. You… you bastard, you bloody bastard.'

'Fuck you, Frenchman.' He snorted, a sort of laugh. His eyes glazed over.

Stiffening his arm, Béart pressed his finger against the trigger. Holding his breath, he urged himself to do it, to kill him, to kill the bastard… But he couldn't. Instead, summoning every ounce of his strength, he swung his boot in, catching the Turk in the ribs.

But the man was already dead.

'Hector? Hector.' The horse had slumped to the ground, lying on his side in the sand. Clambering over, losing his footing in the sand, Béart reached the horse, brushing his forelock from his eyes. 'Hector, what's the matter? What's the matter?'

Hector was panting heavily, occasionally emitting a strange gurgling noise, his eyes awash with fright. Béart ran his hands down his flanks. 'Don't do this to me, Hector; we've come too far for it to end like this. Please, Hector, get up, eh? Stop this, will you? I'll get you some water. That'd be nice, hey?' He slipped the bit from the horse's mouth, loosened his girth and tried to brush off the worst of the sand. It was then he noticed it. 'Oh, shit. Oh, shit, no…' A circle of blood on his hindquarters attracting vile little flies. 'Please, God, no…' The enormity of what'd he done hit him like a kick in the stomach – one of his stray bullets had caught him. 'Oh, God, I'm sorry,' he sobbed, burying his face into Hector's neck. 'I'm sorry, Hector, I'm sorry…'

And there he remained, for how long he didn't know, but the sun had fully risen, burning into the back of his neck. Hector was dying, but he was dying slowly. His whole body quivered continuously, his mouth frothed up with discharge and bile. He was in agony. Béart wanted to cry but no, he had to remain strong, even if just for another few moments.

He checked the revolver barrel – two bullets left. One each, he thought. He swallowed. This time, he knew, he only had the one chance – if he lost his nerve, he'd never get it back again. He kissed the horse over the eye, tasting the sand and dirt. He tickled the horse's ears. This time there was no grin. He clicked the revolver.

'Just think, eh, Hector. Soon you'll be in that field. The one with all the girly horses to keep you company in your old age. Think of all that moist grass, as much as you can eat, and there'd be a river; yes, a river with cold, fresh water. That'd be nice, wouldn't it? The sun will shine, a nice sun, not like this one, and you can shade under the trees.' He pressed his finger against the trigger. 'And after the war, after all this is over, I'll come and visit you. Yeah? I promise I'll visit you every day. It'd be perfect, eh? Everything will be just perfect, my friend.' The horse looked up at him, his huge black eyes reflecting the sun. He seemed to know. 'My dear friend...'

And then he squeezed.

*

Henri Moreau considered Roger Béart. 'You shot an unarmed man in the back.'

'It wasn't like that.'

'Sounds like it.'

'So what? I shot him. I had to; I had no choice.'

'Someone who could have provided useful intelligence to your commanders? Whatever the circumstance, doesn't sound right to me.'

'Leave him be, Henri,' said Gustave Garnier.

'And what would you have done, eh?' asked Béart.

'Shot the horse down and kept the Turk alive.'

'I did shoot the horse; I just didn't mean to. I loved that horse, I really did, you know...'

'And then a patrol found you?' asked Antoine Leclerc.

'Yeah.' Béart sighed. 'I was ready to put a bullet through my head but, yeah, they found me – and they found the Turk too.'

'And you say this was in 1917, Roger?' said Garnier. 'Over fifty years ago. Yet it still hurts a little?'

Béart nodded.

'Of course, it does,' said Leclerc. 'Time doesn't always heal. Perhaps I've been luckier than most. If you want, I'll tell you my tale now. I promise it has a happy ending!'

The Architect's Story

Drancy, northwest of Paris, February 1944

I lay on my bunk of straw, shivering, staring up at the wooden slats of the bunk above me. Another day of lethargy, of boredom and hunger, laced with the constant anxiety lay ahead of me. I'd been here five months now. I'd been here so long, I'd almost forgotten what my old existence was like. This was my life now, a hut containing a hundred and eighty men, Jews, like me, despised and condemned by society. And God, we were hungry, the undertow of constant pain, the eternal emptiness.

Once, not so long ago, I'd been a pillar of the community, an architect, no less, albeit a junior one, but respected nonetheless, revered. But it was the life that belonged to someone different, someone rather arrogant, a man who took things for granted, a man who floated through life feeling slightly superior. I can look back at myself now and see just how foolish a man I had been. We can never take anything for granted in this life for we never know when the rug will be pulled from under our feet. The man who slept above me was, or rather, had been, a farm labourer, the man above him, an unemployed layabout, a lazy, no-good layabout. Once upon a time, I'd never have spoken to such men, we had nothing in common, or, if we did, I'd go to great lengths not to find it. But here, things are different. I soon learnt to cast aside my prejudices and embraced them, not for what they did, or didn't do, but as men, as worthy and as fallible as me. I have discarded my cloak of superiority, thrown away my conceit for I have such affection for these men now, much more so than I had for my friends in my previous life. There, friendship was based on what we could do for each other; its foundation was built on the self. Here, we are simply friends, the best of friends. We are brothers. We are a community here, one based on true comradeship, a community of the damned. We are lambs here.

I shall never forget the day, the first day of February, the year 1944. I hadn't seen my wife or my mother for weeks. They kept us apart at Drancy. I just hoped they were still together, keeping each other company, keeping each other alive. Five in the morning, we were called up on roll call. I forced myself up from my bunk, my limbs heavy, my mind fogged over with fatigue. We all said good morning to each other. We may have been living in conditions that would shame a pig, but we tried so hard to maintain our standards, saying good morning to each other, saying, 'after you' if we bottlenecked at the door. We all looked so old. Deprivation ages a person like nothing else. We were all gaunt, rake thin with yellow skin, ragged beards, hollow eyes. They never gave us any heating in those huge huts but with so many of us crammed in, it somehow maintained a slither of warmth. We traipsed out into the courtyard in our flimsy overalls and almost buckled under the onslaught of the severe, biting cold.

We stood, backs straight, eyes up, looking straight ahead. Woe betide any man who failed to do so. We had to fight against our weakness, the hollowness of our insides. We were surrounded by guards, several with dogs, keeping their beady eyes on us. A French guard, wrapped in a thick coat, a scarf and a pair of warm gloves, called out our names one by one. And one by one, we answered, confirming our presence. The whole process took an hour. An agonising wait in the piercing cold. At the end of this torturous routine, they read out any special announcements – a new regulation, orders from the Germans, a change to our already meagre diets, that sort of thing. But the worst, the thing we all dreaded, was the announcement of the next transport out of here. Then, we waited with bated breath as they read out the names of those slated to be on the next train – a "change of residence". So far,

I'd been lucky but I knew, as we all did, it was just a matter of time. And today, the first of February, it *was* my turn – I heard my name ring out across the courtyard. Antoine Leclerc. It seemed to hover on the breeze, echoing in my mind. I let out a little cry, too quiet to be heard by the guards, but a cry, nonetheless. I clenched my fists and stretched my jaw.

The guard continued. 'Those allocated for the next transport are to gather their things and report back here in two hours. Latecomers will be shot.' He paused to allow this little aside to sink in. I'll be late, I thought. Surely, better a bullet here than what waited for me at the other end. We were dismissed. Slowly, we all made our way back to our barracks. Once inside, we hugged each other and stamped our feet, trying to warm ourselves up. We had two hours. That meant we still had time for breakfast. Of course, 'breakfast' was a euphemism. A black tea and the smallest, hardest slab of bread imaginable. I would hold that piece of bread and every day decide how I wanted to eat it – whether to nibble at it and prolong the ecstasy or whether to swallow it down in two or three mouthfuls simply for the momentary joy of something small but tangible in my stomach.

After our meagre breakfast, we returned to our huts, as usual, but this was different – because I knew I'd never do so again. I gathered my two items – a comb and a tiny book of stories by Voltaire. That was the total sum of my possessions.

I placed the black comb against my top lip, clicked my heels and threw my arm out. My companions laughed heartily as if they'd never seen me do my Hitler impersonation before. Such simple pleasures. And then it was time to say goodbye. I looked at my unemployed, layabout friend and said, 'You... you are a disgrace, an absolute scoundrel.'

'Yeah,' he said. 'But I know you love me like a brother.'

And at that moment, I almost burst into tears because, damn him, he was right. I did love him. I hugged him. 'I'll miss you,' I said.

'I'll miss you too, you stuck-up snob.'

He kissed me on the cheek.

'Look after yourself,' I said. And with that, I left.

I met my doomed companions outside, under the grey-leaden sky, maybe up to a thousand men, women and children. I shivered. It wasn't so cold now but malnutrition left us all vulnerable to the cold. I hadn't seen a woman from close-up for months. Maybe, just maybe, Madeleine might be here, my mother too. I knew I had a couple of minutes before they called us to order, so quickly, I skirted around, pushing people aside, searching, searching... I wasn't the only one; everyone was searching for a loved one, shoving others out of the way in their desperation, shouting names. It's astonishing, I thought, how people, so weakened, can find such incredible strength. I was one of them. I didn't want to see them, my

107

gorgeous wife, my beloved mother. I so didn't want to see them, to know that they, like me, were about to embark on their final journey, but at the same time, I'd have given up my soul to see either of them one final time. And then I did see them, both of them, together, holding hands. My heart tumbled. I tried calling out my wife's name, but it died on my lips. She looked so much older, so haggard, so filthy, so diminished, yet beautiful, still beautiful, as beautiful as the day I first saw her, so many, many years ago, the day I fell in love with her. And I saw her today as if seeing her for the very first time, and my heart somersaulted as I fell in love all over again. My wife, my beautiful wife. 'Madeleine? Madeleine...'

She turned on hearing my voice. She looked at me as if I was a stranger to her. I could see the confusion, the panic almost, in her eyes. It took a few seconds for her eyes to focus, to realise it was I, her husband, standing before her. I knew why – I also had changed almost beyond recognition. 'Antoine? Is that... is that you?'

'Madeleine.'

'Oh, my god, Antoine.' We fell into each other's arms and embraced tightly, breathing in the scent of the other, thankful to have found one another. She was wearing a dark blue cardigan and a cheque skirt.

'I never thought I'd see you again,' she said, swallowing her tears. 'Oh, my darling, my sweet darling, I've not stopped thinking of you.'

I loved her so much. They could destroy us physically, even spiritually, but no one could destroy love, a love such as ours.

I turned to say hello to my mother. I couldn't speak. My poor mother. 'Mama...'

'Is that really you, Antoine?' She didn't say the words, she mouthed them. She had no voice left. I wrapped my arms around her and tried not to shudder at the feel of her bones. Her watery eyes were lost in a haze of greyness, her hair was brittle, her skin like parchment. She could barely stand, leaning heavily on a stick.

I took her delicate hand and rubbed my fingers over her dry, paper-thin skin. I glanced up at Madeleine. She shook her head. My mother, in her early sixties, looked like a hundred. How could she have aged so much in five short months? But, of course, I knew the answer. These months have been anything but short. They had been the longest five months of our lives. Anxiety is a killer; when anxiety is extreme, when its everyday presence eclipses everything else, it can kill the spirit, the person.

'What's happened to you, Mama?' I said it, then at once regretted it. I had no need to ask; it was obvious. The answer lay in one word – *Drancy*.

My mama smiled but it came out as a grimace, and her teeth.... Oh god, her teeth.

I turned to Madeleine. 'She can't get on that train,' I said in a whisper. 'It'll be the death of her.'

'I know, Antoine. I've pleaded with them, but...'

'But?'

'You know what they're like. They don't care.'

A magnified voice cut through our conversations. An authoritative voice, bringing us to order; ordering us to stand in orderly lines. I took my mother's hand.

It all happened so quickly, the brutal efficiency of death. Its finger hovered over us as we were organised and placed into groups and then shuffled onto a bus, one of many. I helped Mother up onto the bus and made sure she had a seat. I sat next to her; Madeleine behind. The bus soon filled. People sniffed and cried. Children held onto their mothers, their eyes shot through with fright. No one spoke. It took an age to load everyone on but eventually, we were ready, and the convoy of buses trundled through the gates of Drancy and out onto the open road.

We passed through the grey countryside, fields of grey stretching into the distance. Faraway buildings, houses with smoking chimneys. We overtook a horse and cart, the driver waving incongruously as each bus passed. The bus transported us just three kilometres south to the railway station in the town of Bobigny. The station had been closed before the war but the Germans had reopened it specifically for their transports from Drancy. By the time we arrived, it was still only nine o'clock in the morning.

The train was waiting for us, a battered-looking locomotive and, behind it, several wagons, perhaps as many as twenty-five. Dotted around the place stood numerous French and German guards with their dogs, awaiting our arrival. We were ordered off the bus. I held onto my mother's hand, stroking it, trying to calm her. Madeleine took her other arm. 'Hurry up,' shouted one of the guards as I helped Mother navigate the steep steps off the bus. 'Hurry up.'

The guards shoved us from the buses to the awaiting train, yelling at us, abusing us. 'Quicker, quicker. Move on, move on. Hurry, hurry.' We, the passengers on our bus, were told to get on one of the central wagons. They'd placed a plank against the wagon to make it easier for the old and the weak, like my mother, to get on. Madeleine went first and helped me steer my mother up, my mother using her stick. 'Give me your hand, Agnès. That's it.'

Everywhere, the same shouts: 'Up, up, up.' My book by Voltaire fell out of my pocket. I wanted to retrieve it but somehow I was washed along with the surge of people. I could hear Mother talking to herself but such was the noise around me, I couldn't make out her words. A German soldier counted us in.

And so we found ourselves in a wagon car, four wooden

walls, a small, grilled window at the front end, a bit of straw strewn around and two buckets, one full of water, the other empty. I reckoned the wagon to be about twenty-five feet by eight. Nowhere to sit. I leaned Mother against the wall as others joined us, one after another after another. It quickly got crowded in there as more and more people were forced inside. 'How many more?' asked Madeleine. Soon people were squeezing against me, and still they kept coming, more and more and more. People were shouting, 'Move up, move up, make room.' 'There *is* no more room.' 'Shift yourself, will you?' 'Move up.' I kept my eye on my mother. Madeleine and I tried shielding her. My heart was thumping against my chest as the true realisation hit home – we were going to be crammed in like this for hundreds and hundreds of miles, for two, three, maybe four days. Surely, *surely*, they can't do this to us. My poor mother. She needed comfort, a seat, anything but this barbarity. I just couldn't see how we could survive this, my mother especially. A German voice shouted at us. 'There're a hundred and two of you in here. Whether dead or alive, you make sure there's a hundred and two at the other end.'

And then they closed the doors, plunging us into darkness save for the shaft of light from the rectangular window. People screamed. Someone vomited, causing more people to move. I could hear more doors closing further down the track, one after another. The Germans outside continued shouting and bellowing instructions – at us, at the French, at each other.

A man within the wagon raised his voice. 'Friends, please, calm yourselves.' The voice belonged to Rabbi Drucker. I could just about make him out, a yellow armband around his upper sleeve – the Germans had designated him as our overseer. 'We must maintain calmness, for all our sakes.'

'You want us to be calm?' said a woman's voice from the far side of the wagon. 'In here?'

'I know it's difficult but there're so many of us. We have a long journey in front of us; we must cooperate, we must help each other during our darkest time.'

'Oh, we're cooperating all right. We always do what the Germans tell us.'

'We have a couple of functionaries with us with a small supply of medicine for those who need it. The Germans have also supplied them with bread which we must ration strictly and fairly.'

Bread. Even the word was enough to make me salivate.

Nothing happened for a while, how long I don't know; I was already losing my sense of time. The wagon fell quiet save for the occasional whimpering, but no one spoke. It was as if we were all holding our breaths, waiting, just waiting. Slowly, my eyes grew accustomed to the dark. I could see things now, make faces out. Madeleine took my mother's stick and gently eased her down and sat her on the wooden floor. Her matchstick-like legs looked so vulnerable and exposed. What if someone stepped on them? They'd snap and break.

Finally, the train jerked into life. A fresh cry went up, from our carriage and all the carriages on either side. This was it, the start of our final journey.

I broke out into a sweat, aware of it creeping down my back, tickling my skin. My mouth had gone dry, my tongue stuck to the roof of my tongue. I knelt and took hold of my mother's hand. Someone stepped back and pushed me over. I scrambled over to protect my mother's legs. I glanced up to see a small girl of about five clinging to her mother's legs, her face wet with tears.

The train gathered speed. We were on our way. Destination unknown, our fate unknown. People were humming. Rabbi Drucker was leading with a hymn, his toneless voice grating on my ears. After a while, people began talking. The general consensus was that we were being transferred to Poland to work. 'Listen,' I heard a deep-throated man say to all who could hear them. 'I had a few francs on me, and a couple of Germans got me to hand them over and gave me a receipt in return. Look...' I saw his hand waving a piece of paper above his head. 'They said once we were in Poland, I could give this receipt to the council of elders and get the same value in Polish money, minus a little for commission.'

Someone laughed. 'And you believed them, did you?'

'Yeah, why not? They need the labour in Poland.'

I looked at my mother. There'd be no way Mother could work.

Madeleine knelt beside me. 'How is she?'

'Not good.'

She stroked my face. 'I've missed you, Antoine.'

I tried to smile. 'I've missed you, too.'

I looked at her and for the briefest of moments I saw again the woman I'd fallen in love with all those years ago; I saw the gleam in her eyes, the shine of her oh-so-black hair, her soft voice and gentle soul. We met in a cafe near Notre Dame. I was a student, politics my subject, Madeleine a waitress. It was the summer of 1939. That first time, I went in with some friends, and I fell in love with the pretty, smiley waitress the moment I saw her. I returned the following day, this time by myself. I barely had two centimes to rub together but I simply had to see her. I must've had 'impoverished' written all over me because, unrequested, she served me a pastry and put her finger to her lips. To my young, over-enthusiastic self, I decided this, in itself, was a declaration of love. I simply had to ask her out. Each time I went, I was determined to do so, and each time, my nerve failed me. In the end, *she* asked me out. We went to a bar in the Latin Quarter one evening, and we talked and we drank and we laughed. It remains the happiest evening of my life. Six months later we were engaged but we never had a chance to marry. Six months after that, Germany invaded and France fell. We never had chance to have children. And right now, on this cramped wagon heading east, I am thankful.

Madeleine curled my mother's legs up, so they weren't so exposed. I stood up and felt my knees creak. I am old before my time. Rabbi Drucker was now chanting the psalms of King David and many of my companions joined in, taking comfort from the familiar words, their rhythm. It was horribly hot and claustrophobic inside the wagon, despite the sharp cold wind that blew through the grill of the open window.

I needed to relieve myself. I elbowed my way through to the corner of the wagon, apologising as I inched my way forward. An older couple had taken it upon themselves to hold up a blanket, shielding the person using the bucket, offering them a degree of privacy. I took my place in the queue. Of course, it was that much more difficult for the women. I noticed the second bucket, the one with our water, had been kicked over. My insides tightened at the thought of surviving in this wagon for so long without water. I smiled at a wiry-haired woman as she emerged from behind the blanket, her eyes down. I took her place and instinctively my hand went to my nose as I retched. Was this really the way to treat human beings?

The hours passed. The continual pounding of the train thumped through my head. People swayed with the movement

116

of the train. I so wished I had my Voltaire to help me pass the time. The hunger gripped me now, more intense than before. We'd been hungry from the moment France fell to the Germans. We'd complain about the lack of food, of always being hungry. Hell, little did we know that was nothing to what was to come. Hunger robs a person of their spirit; it warps our emotions and renders everything else in our lives meaningless. I often dreamt of food, of lavish banquets, the delight of sharing and enjoying. I'd wake up and howl as the reality hit me. I was still here, I was still hungry, I was still miserable; I was still a Jew.

I felt a tug on my trouser leg. Mother was looking up at me and with her hand beckoned me down. I knelt beside her. I am tall, so it wasn't easy. Madeleine joined us. Mother said something but her voice was too fragile to hear. I shuffled closer and put my ear next to her mouth.

She took my hand. 'Remember Me Me?' she said in her hoarse voice.

'Me Me?' That was the name of my uncle's cat. 'Yes, of course.'

'The chimney.' Her eyes shot up, focusing on something high behind me. I turned around. Mother was looking at that small grilled window.

When I was about fourteen, my uncle's cat got stuck up a chimney and I climbed up and rescued her. I was thin and good at gymnastics. I enjoyed the challenge, keen to earn adult praise. I came back down, covered head to toe in soot with a small, filthy ginger cat in my arms. Indeed, I was the hero of the hour. My uncle never forgot and frequently called me Antoine the Adventurer from that point on.

'Oh my God,' said Madeleine. 'Your mother wants you to jump, Antoine.'

'What?'

'Through the window.'

My mother took Madeleine's hand. 'Both of you.'

'No, Agnès. We can't leave you on your own.'

I shook my head. 'No. No way.'

Mama pulled me closer. 'Please, Antoine. I am dying. I can die happy if I know you live.'

I tucked a loose strand of her hair behind her ear. 'You're asking too much, Mama.'

'Live for me, Antoine.' I knew talking was costing her, draining her of what little strength she had left. 'Have children, Antoine. Be happy. Both of you. Please live. For me. For my… for my grandchildren.'

I had to look away. I held my breath, trying to calm myself. I looked at Madeleine. She nodded at me. She wanted us to do it. I looked up at the window. Could I climb that high? Did I have the strength any more? I was certainly thinner than I used to be. And what about Madeleine? Could she? But no, it was out of the question; I simply couldn't leave my mother to face the darkness that lay ahead of her.

'I can't, Mama. I can't.'

She squeezed my hand. 'You must. I have lived a good life, my son. A good life. It's your turn now. You are my only child; you must do as I say.' She wanted to say more, I could tell, but her voice was taken by a fit of coughing.

Madeleine and I stood up.

We gripped hands. 'Madeleine–'

'We must. For her sake, Antoine, we must.'

Antoine the Adventurer. I remembered jumping down onto the hearth with this mangy cat in my arms, her coat covered with dirt, my clothes, my hair, caked in it too. My uncle clapped his hands in delight, and my mother gazed at me with wonderment, her head tilted to one side, a small smile playing on her lips, and I knew at that moment what it was to be loved. I looked down at my mother now and realised she was gazing up at me with that same look, the same expression of love, and I knew then what I had to do.

Madeleine knelt again, put her arms around my mother and kissed her cheek. I heard her whisper, 'Thank you, Agnès.' Madeleine stood up, the tears streaming down her face.

It was my turn. 'Mama–'

'Go, Antoine, my boy, go now. And remember…'

'Yes, Mama?'

She swallowed. 'Remember, I love you. I shall always love my adventurous little boy.'

My heart fell apart. I opened my mouth to tell her I loved her too but the words, stuck in my throat, wouldn't come. She squeezed my hand. There was no need to say it; she knew.

Madeleine helped me to my feet. I could hardly see her; she'd become but a blur. I wiped away my tears with the heel of my hand. Madeleine put her arms around me. 'We must do it straight away,' she whispered. 'While the train's still in France or Belgium.'

She was right; once we were in Germany, it'd be too late; no one would give us shelter in Germany. It had to be now.

'Are you sure you can do it?' I asked.

'No. Are you?'

I looked at the rectangular window. It'd be a squeeze, for sure, and it was fairly high up. 'No. But we have to try.'

I looked down at my mother one final time. I couldn't risk bending down and kissing her; I knew if I did, I'd never leave her. A smile passed across her lips as she blew me a kiss, and for a moment I saw her, not as the emaciated woman the Germans had made her, but a younger, vibrant, loving woman, a mother who loved me very much.

I felt a hand clasp my wrist. I looked down at a blonde-haired woman, a raw gash across her cheek. 'Are you jumping?'

I nodded yes.

She grinned at me, exposing a set of blackened teeth. 'Good luck to you, son. May God be on your side.'

'Thank you.'

Madeleine led the way. It took an age to carefully, forcibly, make our way to the front end of the carriage. When people are so tightly squeezed in together, they don't like being moved. They assumed, I guessed, that we were heading for the bucket. Finally, we got there. Another couple had taken over on blanket duty. Someone was using the bucket, crouched behind the blanket, the sound of their ablutions embarrassingly loud and, despite the roar of the train, all too clear.

I reached up and touched the grill. I was one point eight metres tall, but I knew I wasn't tall enough to get enough purchase to remove the grill. Madeleine shook my arm. 'Antoine, stand on the bucket.'

'The bucket?' I realised she meant the overturned water bucket. She reached down and passed it to me. The additional height was all I needed. I could get my slim fingers through the holes in the grill but when I pulled, I knew I'd never remove the grill.

'Hey!' came a voice near me. 'What are you doing?'

'We're going to jump,' said Madeleine, matter-of-factly.

'You can't do that. That's not fair.'

'He's right, that's not on.' said another voice, a woman's. 'You heard what they said. They have to count a hundred and two of us at the other end, else there'll be hell to pay.'

'Like there isn't any way,' said a third voice.

The whole wagon, or so it seemed, engaged in this. Meanwhile, I quietly removed my pullover and my shirt. Holding my shirt, I put my pullover back on. I threaded the tail end of the shirt through one of the central holes within the grill and pulled. I was not as strong as I used to be, but I thought if I put my every ounce of strength into this, I could possibly do it.

Meanwhile, around me, the argument raged. 'You listen to too many rumours. They're putting us to work, so we need to prove ourselves useful to them.'

'On the amount they feed us?'

The shirt ripped. I fell back, pushing over a couple of others, like a row of dominoes. Straightening ourselves, one of them said, 'You need to soak the shirt in piss.'

'What?'

'Seriously, it'll strengthen your grip.'

'You sure?'

'Horrible, I know, but trust me.'

I didn't want to trust him. I tried again, looping the shirt through the grill and slamming my foot against the side of the wagon. I could sense a bit of give but not enough, nowhere near enough. Frustrated, I tried to block out the shouting. Madeleine seemed ensconced in this and I knew why; she wanted to focus people's attention on her, leaving me to quietly get on. I could hear Rabbi Drucker trying to call order but failing to do so. After two attempts, I knew my strength, such as it was without food, was failing me. Damn it, living was more important than my squeamishness. I took the shirt and plunged it into the bucket now full of urine and excrement. I screamed as my eyes watered. I fell back, clutching my chest, retching. Someone helped me to my feet. Again, I threaded the now sodden and stinking shirt through the grill. Again, I braced myself with one foot against the wagon wall. This was it; it had to come off this time. Just had to. I took a deep breath. The argument ceased as quickly as it'd begun. Everyone was watching me, some willing for me to succeed. I caught Madeleine's eyes. I thought of my mother and, gathering all my strength, pulled. I could feel the grill loosening. Someone came and joined me. Together, we pulled, clenching our teeth, our eyes closed. A small cheer erupted as the grill came flying off and my companion and I fell back into a heap. We'd done it!

Rabbi Drucker held up his hand. 'We have decided. All those who want to jump, may do so. But, be warned, it will be dangerous.'

No one, not a single soul, responded. I looked at Madeleine.

We were to be alone in this. That was fine, a pity, but fine. 'Do you want to go first?'

'No,' she said. 'You go.'

'Let me go say goodbye to my mother again.'

'No.' She stopped me. 'It'll only make it worse for her. Go now.'

I nodded. 'Once I'm outside, don't hesitate.'

'Antoine…'

'Yes?'

'I love you.'

I wanted to hug her, to kiss her, but, my hands stinking of piss, I couldn't do it.

Two men offered their interlocked hands as a footrest. I thanked them. I placed my left foot into their cupped hands. 'Let's go,' I said, trying to give myself courage. They hoisted me up. The gap was tight, of course, but I was so thin now. I pulled myself halfway through. The blast of air hit me, causing my eyes to water again. Balancing half-in, half-out of the window, I dragged my left leg up. I clung on, tottering on the edge, as I brought up my right leg. Then, holding onto the splintered edge of the window, I lowered myself onto the coupling that held the two wagons together. The wind whipped at me, making it difficult to breathe, my cheeks wobbled. It seemed incredible that the train, pulling so many wagons, could go so fast. The countryside passed in a blur; my clouded vision unable to make any sense of it. It was still morning; I could tell from the light. I had to jump, had to do it now. I knew I could be jumping to my death; God knows where I could land. But there was no turning back now. I had to do it.

With my heart pounding, I leapt. A second later, I hit the ground, winding myself badly. Lurching forward, I rolled and rolled, only coming to a stop as I hit a silver birch. I felt no pain apart from my winded stomach. I staggered to my feet; so dizzy my legs almost gave way. The train shunted away from me, spewing steam, the last wagon rumbling past, the railway track buzzing. It seemed to be going so slowly from this angle. Had I really done it? Yes, I had! I'd jumped the train – I was free!

But my euphoria lasted but a second or two – for where was Madeleine? I squinted, desperate to see her. Where was she? Had she jumped? I resisted the urge to call out, I couldn't attract attention, although, God knows, it felt like the middle of nowhere here, just the steep bank to the right of me, leading up to the railway tracks, and, to my left, fields and a few trees under a leaden sky. The train disappeared around a bend in the track. I could still hear it, rapidly diminishing as it took my mother away from me.

I caught my breath. I began to walk on a stony path that ran along the bottom of the bank, my eyes peeled for Madeleine, my every sense alert to the slightest danger. Maybe she hadn't made it, maybe she hadn't been able to climb up to the window, maybe she'd lost her courage. I wouldn't have blamed her. I must have walked half a kilometre when I saw, lying on the damp grass, a shoe. I picked it up. It was still warm; it was Madeleine's. I looked around, calling out her name. 'Madeleine? Madeleine, where are you?'

'I'm right behind you, Antoine.'

I spun around, and let out a little cry – there she was, dishevelled, her face streaked with dirt, out of breath, but beaming; my wife, my beautiful wife.

*

Paris, September 1957

Our daughter enjoyed playing football. Where she picked up this interest, I don't know. It was a warm September evening, the first hint of chill making its presence felt. Madeleine and I sat on a bench in our local park watching Agnès play. It was difficult for her; most boys pushed her away. After all, football was a boy's game, not one for girls. But here, in this park, she'd found a group of boys who not only accepted her but also recognised, reluctantly at first, her ability. I watched her play, my chest swelling with pride, while Madeleine, next to me, read her novel, her eyes shielded by her straw hat.

Twelve years had passed; twelve years of happiness. Madeleine and I married as soon as the war ended. We had no family present, no friends. Everyone we knew had been blown out of our existence, scattered God knows where. Many, I presumed, had perished. But we had survived. Most days, it was a matter of joy; we'd escaped death and come out the other side, scarred but grateful to be alive. Other days, it proved harder to take. I'd left my mother to face the end alone. I should have stayed with her, held her hand. But I hadn't. I'd chosen life. Often, I dreamt about the train. I dreamt of the people, all squashed in together, the panic, the fear of what lay ahead. I'd awake, drenched in sweat. Madeleine held me, telling me to breathe, that everything was fine, that she loved me.

Agnès was born a year later. We named her after my mother. And from the moment I first laid eyes on her pink, chubby face, I knew I'd done the right thing. The nightmares stopped.

A cheer erupts. Agnès has scored a goal. Damn it, I missed it; I should've been concentrating more. I take to my feet and applaud. Madeleine pulls me down by the tails of my jacket. 'Sit down, you fool. No one else is clapping.'

I sit. She leans over and kisses my cheek to show she means no ill feeling. I take her hand. Often, when Agnès was still small, we'd talk of how lucky we were, how proud my mother

127

would have been of us, of her granddaughter. We rarely say it now; we have no need to. A smile, a kiss, a squeeze of the hand is all that is necessary.

The game has finished. Pullovers and tracksuit tops are gathered, the ball kicked back to the boy who owns it. They shake hands, all very formal. Agnès jogs over to us, her cheeks flushed, her ponytail coming loose. 'Good goal, Agnès.'

'Not really. It got a lucky deflection.'

I kiss the top of her head.

'Hungry?' asks Madeleine.

'Starving.'

'I'm not surprised,' I said. 'Come on then, let's get going.' I buttoned my coat, pleased we were heading home.

As we were leaving, Madeleine suggested buying Agnès an ice cream. She then bumped into someone she knew from school, a fellow teacher. The two of them exchanged pleasantries while Agnès stroked the woman's dog, a little black poodle. The woman had a bit of gossip she wanted to share with Madeleine, something about a colleague's indiscretion. Subtly, Madeleine pulled her towards the ice cream van, Agnès and the dog following.

I hung back, feeling slightly self-conscious. It was then that I sensed a presence near me, a shadow encroaching over me. I turned and stepped back a pace on seeing an elderly woman in a camel coat standing stock still, staring intently at me.

128

Unnerved, I opened my mouth to ask her if she was OK. But the words slid back down my throat. She was as tall as me, surprisingly bright crimson lipstick for an older woman, I thought. She stood there, still as a statue, tightly clutching a purple handbag, her fingers playing with its clasp. I knew this woman, I was sure; I'd met her before but where? When? The memory eluded me. The world silenced around us, it was just her and me. I could vaguely hear Madeleine and her colleague queuing for the ice cream, could vaguely hear the poodle yelping, but it was this older woman who held me entranced, her eyes boring into mine, her eyebrows crossed. She too tried to speak but could not. She took a tentative step forward, her shadow at my feet. She took a deep breath, her eyes not leaving me for a second. And then, finally, she spoke. 'You were on the train.'

'Yes.'

'I've been looking for you these last twelve years.' I heard the tremor in her voice. 'I always knew this day would come.'

'Who are you? Were you also on the train?'

She pulled her coat sleeve up and I caught a glimpse of the tattooed number on the inside of her arm.

'After you and your wife jumped, I held your mother's hand. She lost consciousness. But as we approached the end of the journey, she opened her eyes and looked around. She asked where you were. I told you you'd jumped. Her hand gripped mine like a vice. She told me that whatever happened, I had to stay alive and find you – however long it took, she said. I had to find you and deliver this message. I've searched for you all these years. Everywhere I've been, I've been looking for you. I made a promise to your mother. I had to keep it. And I find you here, just a hundred metres from where I live.'

'What did she say? What was her message?'

The woman stepped closer, holding out her hand. I took it.

'She wanted to know she was happy that you'd jumped, happy that you'd decided to live. Her last words were…' She faltered, and pulled her hand away, wiping a tear that had formed in the corner of her eye. 'Her last words were "I can die in peace now".'

I stared open-mouthed at this strident woman in front of me, and mouthed the words, 'She said that?'

'Yes. Yes, she did. And then, sure enough, she died. She died just as we were approaching the gates.'

'Was it Auschwitz?'

'Yes, it was Auschwitz.'

'She never saw it?'

'No. She died in time.'

I spun away as something seemed to suck the air out of my body. My mother never saw it, never saw Hell. She'd been spared, oh thank the Lord, she'd been spared. I turned back to the woman. 'Thank you. Thank you so much for finding me, for telling me.'

'I'm pleased I have. I can rest easy now.' With that, she turned and walked briskly away. I wanted to call after her, to ask her to wait, to tell me more. But I realised there was nothing else to say. I watched her until my eyes blurred with tears, and I could see her no more.

Madeleine and Agnès returned, Agnès licking her ice cream.

'You alright, honey?' asked Madeleine.

I looked at my daughter and my mother's face shone in her face, as clear as anything, and I'd never experienced such a powering sense of love.

Madeleine put her hand on my sleeve. 'Antoine?'

'It's OK,' I stuttered.

'You look upset.'

'No. I'm fine. Truly. Everything's fine now.'

A Time to Say Goodbye

The four men sat back in their chairs, unable to look at each other. The cafe had filled up for lunchtime, almost every table taken, coffees and snacks delivered on trays, a couple arguing, their child under the table playing with a toy car, a group of teenagers dealing cards and smoking. Henri Moreau eyed them with envy. Yes, they had their own pressures, would face obstacles as they made their way in life, but never would they face such injustice, such hardship. His head pounded. Why did everyone have to make so much noise? The children, especially, so damn loud. The smell of coffee, normally so appealing, left him feeling nauseous. He'd regretted telling the others his story. He hoped, after all this time, it'd make him feel better. It hadn't. He should have left it behind; why had he stirred it up? He regretted also hearing *their* stories. Some things are best left unsaid. He thought of his daughter and granddaughter. They'd been on their way from Aix-en-

Provence, taking the train. He couldn't wait to see them, to enjoy their company, their innocent talk.

Garnier pushed his glasses up his nose. 'Is that why you're always so upbeat, Antoine? Because your mother forgave you?'

'Yes, I think it is.'

'A message from beyond the grave,' said Roger Béart, tapping his finger on Garnier's box of matches.

'Absolutely. My life changed that day, the day that woman found me. I never saw her again, even though she said she lived near the park. I never knew her name but I think of her often.'

'You were lucky,' said Moreau.

'I'm not sure I'd go that far,' said Leclerc.

'A comfort, then.'

Leclerc thought about this for a moment. 'Yes, you're right. A comfort.'

'I need to go,' said Moreau.

The others looked at him and each other. One by one, they stood.

'It's been good to talk,' said Garnier. 'Get it all out in the open after all this time.'

'Yes, it was a good idea,' said Leclerc. 'Thank you, Roger.'

Béart smiled briefly. 'Not sure it helped.'

'Oh, but it did,' said Leclerc. 'Don't you think so, Henri?'

'Hm? Yeah. For sure.'

The men gathered their coats and the newspapers. Henri adjusted his hat in the mirror bearing the Coca-Cola logo. Together, they walked to the exit, thanking Jean as they passed, a parade of silent men amongst the noise and clatter of cafe life. They stood outside, adjusting to the cold, a circle of awkwardness. They shook hands with each other, wished each other well, and said how they all looked forward to meeting up again the following week. Then, they turned and each went their way.

But, unknown to all of them, not one of them turned up the following week. None of them could face seeing the others, thinking that perhaps they'd leave it a week. But the second week came and went, and the third, the fourth. And still, none of them could face seeing the others.

They never saw one another again.

*

Henri Moreau walked home, his hands deep in his pockets, the brim of his hat pulled down. So many thoughts whirling around his head, so many memories, so much guilt. It weighed him down. Today, the 17th October 1968, would have been Marguerite's birthday. The autumnal wind blew up leaves at his feet. He passed the barbers and could see Jacques, the dwarf, standing on his box, still hard at work, still cutting hair.

He passed the Metro station and hoped his wife had had a nice day out, guessing she'd be home at the apartment by now.

He passed the park with its nineteenth-century statue. A boy and a girl were playing with a Frisbee while Dad sat on a bench reading the newspaper. Moreau wondered whether he too had read about the black athletes at the Olympics and read about the music conductor and the trial of the Drancy guard. He wondered what the conductor would do now. Would he survive intact or would it be the end of him? The press was jumping on him now. The war may have ended almost a quarter of a century back but people still loved it when they exposed a collaborator or sympathiser, someone they could pour their scorn on and hang out to dry. The more brutal, the better to bury their own filthy secrets. Many had done much worse during the war. How many could truly hold up their heads and say I have done nothing to be ashamed of? Man is measured by his worst deed. He wished now that he hadn't exposed his darkest secret. It was one thing to have it festering inside, but he'd let it out. They would judge him now, forever more. They might tell people, who in turn… The worst of it was that whenever he tried to conjure up his daughter's face, all he saw was her crumpled figure on the yard at Drancy, the bright red and yellow of her teddy bear lying next to her. And he heard his voice, screaming Marguerite's name, the rawness of it screeching through the air.

He arrived back at their fourth-floor apartment to be greeted by Hetty, purring and wanting attention. Wandering through to the kitchen, he could tell that Isabella had returned and obviously gone out again. He filled up the kettle with cold water and placed it on the gas ring. He opened a tin of cat food. Hetty jumped up on the counter, eager for her dinner. 'Calm yourself, little one. Calm yourself.'

He sat at the kitchen table, head in hands, breathing in the aroma of cat meat. He wondered whether there was something he could do to help Isabella – peel a few potatoes, perhaps, cut up an onion or two. He needed normality, to anchor himself in the everyday and its reassuring mundanity.

Instead, he traipsed through to the bedroom. It smelled, as always, of his wife's perfume, and he allowed himself a smile. He opened the curtains that covered the glass door leading out onto the balcony. The bed had been made, the numerous pillows puffed up. He glanced at the framed cross-stitch featuring the Eiffel Tower; he'd never liked it. He preferred the print above the bed, the one of Pissarro's *Landscape at Pontoise*. He'd always liked the vividness of the trees, the solid buildings of the village and the steep field behind it. A book lay on the round table on Isabella's side, a Georges Simenon. On the chest of drawers, a framed photograph of his daughter and son-in-law and Ruby, his granddaughter, an official sort of photo, taken in a studio. The couple divorced soon after.

He picked up the photo. Suzanne, his daughter, had inherited her mother's Italian genes, all dark-haired and much gesticulating of the hands. As father and daughter, they'd never been close. The matter had entirely been his fault. Poor Suzanne, she'd always lived under the shadow of the sister she never knew, and Suzanne's presence was an everyday reminder of how he, Henri Moreau, had failed so badly. He had never loved her enough, never loved her as a man should love his daughter. But somehow, and for reasons he couldn't understand, let alone articulate, it was different with Little Ruby. It was almost as if, having skipped a generation, he was allowed to love again. And boy, did he love her. He adored his Little Ruby. Although still only three years old, she reminded him so much of Marguerite. The same eyes, that wide-eyed curiosity, the same dimpled smile. He always had to prepare himself for seeing her, made sure he was focussed, in the here and now, that he saw Ruby in front of him, and not a ghost from those dark, unforgiving days. He placed the photo back on the chest. 'Live well, live long, my lovely,' he whispered.

He opened the double doors and stepped out onto the balcony. The day had turned colder. He shivered a little as he gazed over the city and listened to the constant thrum of traffic. The rolling clouds had darkened but the day was still just about clear enough to see the Eiffel Tower in the distance. He looked down onto the familiar street below – the awnings of the shops on the opposite side, the yellow plastic chairs of the cafe, one solitary man sitting there, the cars parked up, a row of scooters. He watched a man walking briskly across the pedestrian crossing, carrying a ladder. He could hear children shouting but couldn't see them. It'd only take a second. And then it'd be over, the years of shame, the tarnished memory of his daughter. If only he hadn't spoken today. It hadn't helped at all, it hadn't rid him of his demons; instead, it'd made things a hundred, a thousand things harder. The demons were crashing into him, he'd exposed his despicable shame and he knew they'd thought poorly of him, as indeed, he'd thought poorly of them. He couldn't stand it any more, the memory of that day, the crack of the rifle shot, the sound of his screaming, her crumpled little body. Living with it, day in, day out, was torture. He hated himself and knew he always would. But he knew he could rid himself of the torment – it'd be easy; it wouldn't take long, just a moment, that was all. Just a moment. Simply swing one leg over the railing, then the other. He was getting old, he was losing his memory, he knew that. It'd only get worse. He'd be doing everyone a favour. It was too much to ask Isabella to nurse him as he became progressively worse. Far better to save her, and to save himself from the indignity.

The railing was too high. Either that, or he was too old now to swing his leg that high. He needed a stool. Returning inside, he took Isabella's bedside table and carried it back outside.

And then he remembered something. Back indoors, he went through to the living room and rummaged through a set of drawers. It was here somewhere, he was sure of it. He pulled out folders of correspondence, old paperbacks and out-of-date passports, throwing them all to the ground, such was his haste. Hetty came to say hello. He pushed her away. He heard next door's toilet flushing. And then he saw it, the fragile brown envelope. His heart quickened. He hesitated, running his finger across the dry texture, trying to find the courage to do something he hadn't done in many, many years. He had to do it; the time had come. Gently, he lifted the flap of the envelope and withdrew the single item inside, face down. His eyes took in his wife's handwriting, his *first* wife. *11 Août 1939*. That was all, just the date, a month before the war. He took a deep breath and held it, aware now of Hetty's contented purring nearby. Slowly, he turned the photograph over. He saw her smiling face for a moment before squeezing his eyes shut. Forcing his eyes open, he tried again. His heart pounded on seeing her face again. The similarity between Marguerite and Ruby was unmistakable; they were so alike. They'd been on a walk in the countryside. Marguerite was only three when he snapped the photo, her windswept hair partially obscuring one eye, her mother's hand resting on her shoulder. He remembered she'd been frightened by a large dog and he had had to carry her for a while. She'd be thirty-three this very day.

What a waste, such a terrible waste. He placed the photo in his jacket's inside pocket.

He glanced down at the pile of papers and books on the living floor. He'd have to clear that up before Isabella returned and before Suzanne and Ruby arrived. First, he needed to close the bedroom door; he could feel the breeze from here. As he passed through the kitchen, he took a box of matches and, cupping his hands, lit the gas ring beneath the kettle.

Back in the bedroom, he looked at the small, stool-like table he'd placed on the balcony. He stood there, the wind ruffling his hair, and stared at it. Time slowed down. Noises from the street far below muffled before fading away. A slim shaft of sunlight broke through the clouds. Carefully, he stepped up onto the stool, hoping it'd take his weight. The top of the railing was now at his waist. A moment's courage, that was all he needed. Just a moment. He stood there for a few seconds, balancing on the stool, his feet squeezed together. He looked down again at the street. A lorry passed, leaving black exhaust fumes in its wake. He retrieved the photograph from his jacket. He ran his finger across her face. 'Marguerite, my love. Marguerite. Marguerite.'

He was only dimly aware of a high-pitched whistle, its shrillness intensifying. The whistle hid the noise of the key in the door, of the door opening. He didn't hear the voices – that of his wife and daughter, wondering why Henri had left the kettle to boil. He kissed Marguerite's face. Still holding onto the photo, he used his hands to hoist one leg up onto the railing. He settled his backside onto it. Just a moment of courage. He held his breath. The bedroom door flew open. 'Grandpapa, Grandpapa.' Ruby's high-pitched voice sliced through him.

'Marguerite? Oh, my darling girl. Is that you, Marguerite?'

Ruby stood at the door of the balcony, a quizzical expression in her eyes. 'What are you doing, Grandpapa?'

'What? Oh! I, er…' Tears sprang to his eyes as he manoeuvred himself off the railing, and off the stool. 'Oh, Ruby, oh how lovely. I'd quite forgotten.'

'Why are you on the rail, Grandpapa?'

He wiped his eyes with the back of his hand. 'Am I? Oh, dear. Wait a moment.' He clenched his eyes shut and tried to catch his breath, trying to bring himself back down to earth.

'Who's Marguerite?' asked his granddaughter.

'Marguerite?' He could barely speak. 'Oh, no one; no one at all. Listen, my love, don't tell your mother, hey?'

She shook her head.

'Good girl. Good girl.'

The photo slipped from his fingers. 'No!' he cried out. A gust of wind snatched it away from his reach. It hovered a moment before floating quickly down and away and away and away. 'Noooo! Marguerite, Marguerite, Margueriiiiite!'

142

DRANCY: Historical note

The first of sixty-four transports from Drancy left on 22 June 1942; the last on 31 July 1944. 64,759 Jews were deported from Drancy, of which approximately 61,000 were sent to Auschwitz-Birkenau. Fewer than 2,000 survived.

Novels by **R.P.G. Colley**:

The Love and War Series
Song of Sorrow
The Lost Daughter
The Woman on the Train
The White Venus
The Black Maria
My Brother the Enemy
Anastasia
The Darkness We Leave Behind
The Mist Before Our Eyes

The Searight Saga
This Time Tomorrow
The Unforgiving Sea
The Red Oak

Rupertcolley.com